HEDGE
of
THORNS

HEDGE of THORNS

SALLY ASH

Goodfellow Press

This is a work of fiction. The events described are imaginary; the characters are entirely fictitious and are not intended to represent actual living persons.

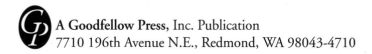

A Goodfellow Press, Inc. Publication
7710 196th Avenue N.E., Redmond, WA 98043-4710

Library of Congress Catalog Card Number 93-080294

Edited by Pamela R. Goodfellow
Cover and book design by Cameron Mason
Cover illustration by Debbie Hanley
Cover photography by Susan Talbott
A special thanks to Nancy Deahl

Printed on recycled paper in the U.S.A.

Every love story
fulfills a dream . . .

One

It didn't start as a fairy tale. There were none of the essential ingredients. In fact, when viewed objectively, it had more the characteristics of a slapstick comedy. They met at a party on Nob Hill, which in itself could have proven extremely helpful, because San Francisco is a city which lays itself open to romance in a big way.

Ben Beresford was in town, visiting his older brother, David, who had a research fellowship at Stanford. Ben was twenty-two at the time, a bit wet behind the ears still, and sporting a pair of wings which told the world that he was a newly qualified pilot. Very newly indeed, although the world need not know that.

David's wife, Jane, welcomed him warmly as a beloved younger brother, and said all the correct, congratulatory things. "And you couldn't have chosen a better moment to appear. We're off to a party this evening, an engagement party actually, and I phoned our hosts to ask if you could tag along. They said they'd be delighted."

Ben didn't think much of phrases like 'tag along'. As third and youngest child in the family it had cropped up quite frequently in his youth, and it suggested definite overtones of nuisance. However, he liked Jane and was on best behavior when around her, so he simply said, "Who's the poor sucker who got hooked?"

"No need to be like that." Jane's voice was calm. "He's a bloke David has come to know through the golf club. Quite revoltingly good looking, in my opinion. Evidently a computer whiz kid. His name is Pete Pendleton, and I gather the family owns everything worth owning round Los Altos. The girl's name is Leigh something-or-other. French sounding. I've only met her once, and that briefly at the club, but I thought she was nice."

Ben thought her tone implied far too nice for Pete Pendleton, but again he refrained from pursuing the suggestion.

It took the three Beresfords about twenty minutes of fruitless and extremely frustrating circling to find a parking space, before they reached the party. By then it was well under way. If the noise level was anything to go by it was already a very successful affair. They could hear the music and bursts of laughter as they waited for the door to be opened. Certainly the bubbly stuff was plentiful and freely flowing, but to arrive knowing nobody and feeling very much a stranger in a strange land, was always hard; and to be stone cold sober when everybody else was two drinks ahead makes the feeling even more acute. Ben was introduced to their hostess, the polished and sophisticated sister of Pete, then to her husband; and to Pete himself.

Ben wondered how old you had to be before people stop labeling you a kid? This bloke must be older than Dave, almost thirty, at least.

"Hi. This is my brother Ben, the pilot." David, he noticed, used that artificial sort of voice one hopes suggests bonhomie. "He only flew in this afternoon."

Pete looked as if he had just skipped out of a fashion ad. Too good looking to be true. He was like a very sleek panther, all purr-y and pleased with himself, with glossy black hair and darkly expressive eyes. The liquid variety about which women swoon. He said, "G'day, mate," in an appalling travesty of an Australian voice, and continued, "Better put another shrimp on the barbie, eh?"

"Hello, and congratulations." Ben wondered if it would upset brotherly relations forever if he said something to wipe that smug expression off the guy's face.

"Congratulations?"

"I thought we were here to celebrate your engagement."

"Oh, that." His grin was openly frank. Nearly a grimace. "Perhaps commiserations would be more the order of the day."

"Then commiserations." Ben replied, mentally smoothing down the prickly hair at the nape of his neck. He turned away to collect the glass of champagne he was offered, thankful for the opportunity. Pete was clearly a first class jerk. He felt rather sorry for the fiancée, wherever she might be in this melee, but no doubt she knew what she was getting herself into.

Anyway, it was hard to see other men through the eyes of women. In his experience, albeit limited, women sought different criteria. There were several occasions when he considered girls of his acquaintance, girls with whom he had grown up, to be throwing themselves away on real creeps. Men like this computer brain box. But when you analyzed the star struck way they reacted in the presence of the adored it became apparent that what he saw and what they saw were chalk and cheese.

Did girls have a similar problem, when trying to understand what made another woman attractive to men? A pity he had no sister to ask, but he might try the idea out on Jane, if the opportunity arose. Tell her it was one of her duties as a sister-in-law. Ask her, perhaps, how she saw Barbara, who was married to his other brother, John.

He wandered away into the large living room, and from there out onto the terrace, collecting a handful of salted cashews, weaving a path through the groups of chattering, laughing people. It appeared to him that everybody present, apart from the three Beresfords, was intimately acquainted with everybody else.

Outside, the air in the June evening was heavy with the scent of summer jasmine, and bright with fairy lights which threaded through the coral colored bougainvillea. He leaned against the balustrade and looked across the city. He didn't know San Francisco well; it was only his second visit to the city, and to America itself, for that matter. But he could recognize Coit Tower outlined against the sky and trace the string of lights which indicated the far shoreline. That dark, rather sinister lump in the water of the Bay had to be Alcatraz.

A girl detached herself from the group of animatedly chattering people standing by the French doors and made her way towards him. "Hi. Do I know you? Or are you a friend of Pete's?"

"Only in a way," Ben replied.

The girl was sort of pretty, maybe meriting six out of ten. Perhaps a little less, certainly not more. Personally, he was into curves in a big way, and she was definitely short changed in that direction. She was wearing a bright red dress and possessed masses of brown curls which cascaded in a vivid jumble round her face and over her shoulders. Her face was a pale oval and it was hard to see her eyes in this light, but at least she looked interested, which was an improvement.

"I'm with the Beresfords, David and Jane. David's my brother, and he's the friend of Pete's. They play golf together. My name is Ben."

"Of course. You're the pilot brother. I'd have guessed at once, if I'd heard you say something."

"Is it as obvious as that?"

"Of course, to Americans. Actually Australia's the flavor of the month over here."

In the light cast onto the terrace through the French doors she turned to him and smiled, a wide, friendly, unambiguous smile. It transformed her, as if a lantern flame had been ignited. It lit her face, it lit the San Francisco night. It lit his heart.

"By the way, I'm Leigh De St. Croix. Pete's my boyfriend; or, as of tonight, my fiancé."

"Cripes!" Ben knew that sounded wet, but it was a great deal better than saying, as his first instinct dictated, are you a raving nutcase? What on earth possessed you to get engaged to that smug, self-opinionated article? "In Australia we're meant to say felicitations to the girl. Is it the same over here? If you say congrats, it's supposed to sound as if you've trapped him into marrying you."

Leigh laughed. "What makes you think I haven't? Trapped him, that is."

Ben felt himself blushing, and knew he was going to make a fool of himself, but instead Leigh saved him by taking his sleeve. "I guess I'd better do a bit more mingling. Let me introduce you to these folks."

After that the party improved and, now that the ice was broken, Ben began to enjoy himself. Leigh didn't stay long with the group to whom she introduced him, but they were all intrigued by Australia and things Australian, had seen the koala ads and plied him for further information. Then food was served, and more champagne, and the whole party took on a different complexion.

He spent a fair amount of time monitoring Leigh's progress about the room, so that now and again he found himself adrift of the conversation surrounding him. He wanted to ascertain whether she had a similar effect on other people, well, blokes, as she had on him. It was hard to tell, because any smile worth anything must contain eye contact, and who could tell that across a room? Or when directed at lesser mortals. As well, she was clearly popular, and this was her evening. She was all the while surrounded by groups of laughing, supportive friends.

Then she moved to a group that was closer, noticed him noticing her, and smiled. Directly at him, directly for him. And again it was as if a fire had been ignited within her which transformed her features and totally altered her face. The result was extraordinary. Once more his heart performed a double backflip, leaped into his throat, hovered there and then, finally, returned to the cavity within his ribs. How could the simple rearrangement of the muscles of someone's face do that? And his anatomy showed every indication of endorsing the behavior of his heart. Ben usually ignored such a response. The general area of his groin was a notoriously poor arbiter of taste, prepared to react lustfully even when rational thought gave it no encouragement.

But not his heart. Never his heart. That part could always be relied upon to be a most trustworthy judge. Until tonight. Tonight it was proving itself a false prophet, taking leave of good sense at complete variance with his brain. The girl was skinny, had too much hair and not a single bulge worth mentioning. This very night she was declaring to the world her attachment to a jerk of the first order. A ratbag, in Australian parlance, who had no more to recommend him than a pretty face. And an ability to do fancy things with computers.

She showed herself to be a poor judge of men.

Jane found him shortly after eleven and indicated that they were ready to leave. By that time so was Ben. He reckoned he had done enough free publicity work for the Great Barrier Reef, TransOz, for whom he flew and Australia in general. Any further and he would be submitting his account to the Minister for Tourism. What was more, he hadn't set eyes on Leigh for eons.

He had also consumed a fair amount of California's best champagne.

He was on his way to find a bathroom, having perceived through a certain fog that he'd better obey the dictates of nature, when he stumbled into one of the bedrooms. He groped for the switch and the darkness was pierced by sudden brightness. Owlishly he focused on the couple in a state of semi nudity who scrambled off the tumbled bed. One was clearly Pete Pendleton, whiz person and fiancé of Leigh, so of course the other one was . . . Leigh, and he'd just not recognized her without the red dress.

It made sense, the engaged couple slipping away for

a spot of groping in private, and Ben was horribly embarrassed at having intruded on their intimacy. Except this girl was blond, and big breasted, and even more embarrassed than Ben. Pete grinned at Ben and casually gathered up the bed cover to hide his unclothed parts. It was the only indication that he recognized himself not entirely in control.

"Well, hi there, kid brother! Kinda caught us. Just saying good-bye to all my yesterdays, if you get my drift. Gotta be a good boy from now on, y'know."

Ben's senses returned to him in overdrive. This piece of junk, Leigh's husband-to-be, was happily screwing some other girl while his fiancée entertained the guests.

It was gut reaction which dictated his next move, and surprise which guaranteed its success. His left fist caught Pete slam in the center of his face and there was a delicious, crunching sound as bone encountered flesh and bone. Had he been privileged to see it, the Physical Education Master at the Sydney Church of England Grammar School for Boys would have whooped for joy.

Pete, whose hands were fully engaged in hiding his naked lower half, was less interested in the artistry displayed by his assailant. He fell backwards into the arms of his blond companion, now wailing hideously, and clutched at his face with the bedcover. Both face and cloth turned a vivid, startling scarlet.

With wits sharpened by the wails and the sight of all the blood, Ben decided that retreat at this moment seemed eminently practical. Even his visit to the bathroom lost its importance. He caught up with Jane and David as they said goodnight, added his thanks to theirs, and followed them into the San Francisco night. As he turned to go he caught a glimpse of a bright red dress near the French doors. He raised a hand, not the one with the grazed knuckles, in farewell. It was hard to tell whether she saw or not.

They did not meet again for five years.

Two

"Ahoy, there."
As Ben let himself in he heard Janna's delighted squeal. "It's Uncle Ben!"

He picked the little girl up as she hurtled into his arms and tossed her into the air amidst more high-pitched squeals and much giggling. She was conceived in America, born in Australia after David's year with Stanford concluded. A Trans-Pacific product.

Jane called from the living room, "Come on in, and go easy on the horseplay. She's just finished her tea." She was wiping the last vestiges of boiled egg from the mouth of two year old Millie who was still confined in her high chair.

The baby moved her face impatiently from her mother's ministrations, held out her pudgy little arms and cried, "Unka Ben! Unka Ben!"

He rewarded such devotion by lifting her carefully out and enclosing her in a warm hug. Then he sat her on his knee and accepted the cup of tea which Jane proffered.

"Dave'll be home soon. He phoned some minutes ago to say he was on his way."

Ben wished, not for the first time, that these favorite people of his lived closer to the North Shore; that it was not nearly a two hour's trek to see them. It was a sentiment echoed by the older generation of Beresfords and had taken on the guise of an old long playing record with a crack in it. But it was useless to complain, because common sense was on their side. Research doctors were not paid the princely salaries of the privileged. North Shore house prices were prohibitive. Their circumstances would improve when Jane returned to the practice after her daughters were in school. Until then they would cut their coat to fit their cloth.

Some time later, after Dave's return, Ben broke his news. The girls had been bathed, read to, kissed and tucked in, the adults spoiled with Jane's sinfully delicious sole Veronique. "I'm off to the States next week. A delivery flight. We take possession of the first of our new 747s."

He said it casually, modestly refraining to point out his delight at having been included in the team to test the new plane and then fly it back over the Pacific. The enormity of the occasion was not lost on his brother and sister-in-law, however.

After all the right exclamations and praise had been accorded Jane said, "Seattle, did you say?"

"Yes. Boeing's plant is up there. Biggest in the world."

His sister-in-law had no interest in Boeing, as long as the airplanes it produced kept Ben in the air and alive. She pursued her own train of thought.

"Do you remember Leigh Pendleton?" Ben shifted a trace uncomfortably in his chair. "She lives there, now. Did I ever mention that? We took you to her engagement party in San Francisco . . ."

Actually, the party had only once been mentioned, briefly, some time after they'd all reassembled in Sydney. The conversation needed some fancy mental footwork on Ben's part.

Jane had brought it up. "That party we took you to. Remember, Ben?"

"I remember getting plastered, and nursing one helluva headache the next day."

David added his six cent's worth. "Evidently, not long after we left, old Pete had some sort of accident. Said he'd walked into a half opened closet door. Sounded a bit fishy to me, even in the dark. And especially when I saw the mess he'd made of his face. Some closet door. Some accident."

Ben refrained from commenting. Jane came unwittingly to his aid. "Mmm. I thought it a bit odd, too. And, you know, I never could warm to that chap. Too self-satisfied by half, although Leigh was a delight."

"But you have to agree he was a pretty sharp golfer," David continued reflectively. "Just an odd number. Only too ready to be chummy before that party, cool as a frosty day, afterwards. I gave up suggesting we might play; put it down to feminine demands. Although I did occasionally see him out on the links."

Jane leaped to defend all womanhood. "Feminine demands, Dave? What on earth do you mean? Selecting dinnerware or P.M.S related?"

David grinned. "Both. Yes, well, some women are like that." And he put up his arms to ward off the cushion hefted at him with some accuracy by his wife.

Now Ben said, "Only Leigh? What about the obnoxious husband?"

"Oh. I never did tell you, did I? He was killed in a car crash, a few months ago. I'm pretty sure they were already living in Seattle, but they can't have been there for long."

"Did you keep in touch, then?"

"Yes. Leigh and I became quite friendly because she asked for my professional advice at one time. We had a couple of lunches together. But no more than that. And we've exchanged Christmas cards ever since we came home. You ought to look her up, if you're in town for more than a few days."

Ben wondered if Leigh had ever heard the true story of the accident. Probably not, unless there had been some other build up provided to explain his assault.

Jane handed David his coffee as she spoke. "Perhaps you can cheer her up, and if nothing else she can tell you what's worth seeing in the area. I assume you don't spend the entire time at the joystick?"

Ben grinned at her. "We don't exactly have joysticks these days. At least not in airplanes. And too much time with the other sort would be awfully tiring. I believe it makes you go blind."

"You adolescent monster!" Jane exclaimed in mock horror. "Why is it that every conversation with you leads to your anatomy?"

■ ■ ■

So it was that Ben came to be standing outside the security door of an apartment block of modest pretension, clutching a bottle of good Australian wine in one hand and

19

some long-stemmed roses in the other. Roses because he really wasn't too sure what was considered correct to offer recently widowed young women and they seemed safe. He had mastered driving on the wrong side of the road, negotiated his way through heavy traffic across a bridge that actually floated, which to him sounded extremely dodgy, managed to follow instructions and leave the freeway at the correct exit. He'd lost himself only twice, and those mere details. He felt he should be awarded Brownie points, or a prize for orienteering.

He also felt rather nervous, as though about to embark on a date. He was only offering a shoulder to a young widow in mourning. Had marriage changed her much? Was she still the girl he remembered? Leigh of the Lovely Smile?

■ ■ ■

Leigh, hearing the bell, asked over the intercom, "Who is it?" She was also feeling surprisingly nervous, but for no other reason than that this was the first time she would be entertaining alone.

"It's me. Ben Beresford. Aussie accent and all."

"Hi. Come on up. Just open the door when you hear it click. I'm on the second floor."

He was sufficiently savvy about America to know that what he called the first floor they would be labeling the second. Where had he read about two people being divided by a single language?

■ ■ ■

Leigh was surprised to hear his voice when he phoned, but she had no difficulty placing him. He was the Australian brother at their engagement party. The pilot who looked so lost upon arrival, like a drop of oil in a pail of water. A nice looking guy. Thick, strong hair bleached blond in that delicious Australian way, tanned and healthy, with the sort of blue eyes one imagined gazing across countless oceans. Seafarers' eyes, had he been born in an earlier century. Well built, too. He had good shoulders, a neat little behind and was the right height. Athletic. Probably something of a jock, she'd thought at the time. He walked with that slight springiness of the ankle which suggests a person quick on his feet.

She sighed. How long ago that evening seemed to be. Part of her distant history. And so much water had passed under the bridge since then. She'd only been a kid herself, just twenty-one. Newly graduated, as innocent of life as a novice nun. Twenty-one and engaged to be married.

Pete was friendly with the other Beresford, the doctor. They played golf together, and David was one of the few golfers who could stretch Pete, so at first they paired up regularly. Then, quite suddenly, David Beresford was O.U.T. Not to be as much as mentioned. Leigh tried to discover why, because she was becoming friendly with Jane, but Pete saw fit not to tell her. Just another of his secrets, in retrospect.

She opened the door to the apartment as she heard footsteps in the hallway. "Hi. Come in. Oh, are these for me? Thank you."

He looked very much as she had remembered. Perhaps a bit taller and a bit broader, but that may have been a trick of memory.

■ ■ ■

There was a strong smell of cat pee in the hallway: the paint was the sort of grayish-white which took years of neglect to achieve. But Ben found the door easily enough. It was opened upon his approach, as if his footsteps echoing on the ugly, worn tiles had penetrated the wall. Then he blinked, thinking for a moment that he must have misunderstood and approached the wrong apartment, that the wrong person was there to welcome him.

What had happened to all those luxurious, tumbling curls? The hair of this young woman was cut in the shortest possible fashion, no more than a sleek, smooth cap of hair. There was just a hint of curl round the ears, no more. And even the bangs could not be called that with any accuracy, but were as clipped as the tonsure of a medieval monk. This person possessed high, finely chiseled cheekbones he'd not noticed before in the perfect oval of her face, and wide, green eyes. Unhappy eyes.

There was more meat on her bones than on the girl he remembered, which suited her; but the smile which greeted him was tight and conventional, and involved only the most fleeting eye contact.

His first reaction was one of panic, because he realized at once that she was not too far away from tears. Was she still in mourning for the caddish husband? If so he was in for one heck of an evening. Why on earth had he listened to Jane?

"Come on in."

Leigh led him into the living room. A small boy was playing on the floor. At sight of Ben he ran to Leigh's side and wrapped himself tightly round her legs. From the folds of her soft denim skirt he regarded the intruder with huge, dark eyes.

"Oh, Peter. Please let go. This is Ben, remember? I told

you he would visit us this evening."

The child peered again at Ben from the safety of his mother's side. He had black, glossy hair and could have been cloned from the cells of his dead father.

Leigh was somewhat embarrassed but clearly not unfamiliar with this mode of behavior. "Punkin, if you hold onto my legs I can't get Ben anything to drink. Why don't you come to the kitchen with me and we'll get you that popsicle I promised?"

The two returned a few minutes later, carrying a tray on which were a beer for Ben, a coffee for Leigh and a popsicle for Peter.

"How's Jane?" Leigh asked. "She sent me a snapshot in her last card, of their little girls. They look adorable. Like two Christmas angels."

"They're all fine." Ben's beer was called Henry's, and was remarkably palatable, a far cry from some of the American brews he had sampled. "The girls are great. I love 'em and just wish I could see more of them. But they live miles out of Sydney." He contemplated the white foam round the rim of the glass. "She forgot to tell me that you had a son."

"Oh. No wonder you looked surprised. This is Peter Sandford Pendleton the Third." She wrinkled her forehead. "Did she tell you about Pete? About the accident?"

"Yes. I'm terribly sorry." That sounded so lame, but what else did one say?

"It was a shock. I guess sudden deaths always are. If a person close to you has an illness or a heart attack you can prepare yourself for the death, and so can they. But an accident's not like that. One minute everything's ordinary, the next there's a cop at the door." She seemed even closer to tears, all big eyes and wobbly voice.

Ben felt horribly embarrassed and wished once more that he was anywhere but in the living room of that small apartment

And it was a very humble dwelling, by any Western standards, but most of all by American ones. Why was she living here? What about all that Pendleton money? What about the parents who owned half the real estate in California? What about the brilliant computer whiz who could command any salary, anywhere?

It didn't add up, not in his reckoning. The silence lengthened.

"I'd intended to invite you out for a meal." He sounded as awkward as he felt. "But I suppose that's not practical, in the circumstances."

"Thanks, anyway." Leigh was getting herself under control again. "It was a nice idea. But I can fix us something after Peter's in bed, if you'd like to stay."

Ben wasn't sure whether he wanted to remain that long, because this was beyond anything his imagination had touched upon. But there was no civilized way to back out without looking like a lout. And, he reasoned, Leigh had probably experienced enough loutishness to last her a lifetime.

She went into the kitchen again for fresh drinks. Ben and Peter were left alone together. Popsicle finished, the little boy had returned to the small cars which he was pushing around a cardboard road. Now he sat back on his haunches and stared at Ben with great, dark eyes from under strongly defined brows. A solemn, almost unblinking stare.

Ben scowled back at him.

He thought suddenly of Janna and Millie, his two little blond nieces; and of Daniel and Su, who were the children of his other brother, John. Great kids. He loved them all. He loved them just for being children, and young, as well as for being part of the family. But not one of them resurrected in him a scene etched for eternity on his mind. Before his eyes flashed a moment in which farce and icy rage and disgust were all interwoven in a tapestry of vivid recollection. And, if he were frank, the memory was not exclusively unattractive. There had been that delectable instant when his fist crunched into a smug face. A face which was, so regrettably, an adult version of this kid's.

And what of that other girl? The one he remembered with the wonderful smile? What had happened to her in those intervening years? To date he'd seen nothing which recalled her to mind at all. That girl appeared to be as dead as her ratbag husband.

Thank goodness the bloody beer was palatable.

Three

hings improved when the kid was out of the way, no longer staring at him with Pete's eyes. Leigh left him with another beer and the news on television, and returned when Peter was tucked into his bed. Ben trailed into the kitchen after her. It was a microscopic box of a kitchen and, like the rest of the apartment, badly in need of a coat of paint. He tried not to get in her way as she prepared a chef's salad for them.

He enjoyed watching women work. Correction: he enjoyed watching efficient women work, and Leigh showed herself to be extremely efficient. There was an economy of movement which pleased him, a neatness about how she cleared away as she went, perhaps dictated by the confined space. They took the bowls of salad back into the living room and ate them at the small dining table. There was a vase of yellow and white daisies in the center. Leigh, making polite conversation, asked him about his career. He told her of his flying experience since their first meeting, his promotions and why he was at present in Washington.

"You mean, Boeing tests a new plane all those hours, then the FAA takes over, and finally TransOz tests it again?"

"That's right. And there's pilot training as well, if it's a new model."

"So you're in town for some time?"

"Could be. It depends how things develop, if there are no hitches. If problems crop up they might send us home until they're sorted out." He rested his arms on the table and steered the conversation away from himself. "Tell me about how you came to be in Seattle."

Leigh was fiddling with the petals which had fallen from one of the daisies. She shrugged. "Oh. Pete was offered a job with Compusoft. They're one of the leading developers of software. So we moved up. We'd been here nearly a year when he . . . when he was killed."

How could he put it delicately? "You've always lived in this apartment?"

Despite the neutrality of his tone she understood. "Of course not! We had a place up in Redmond, in the hills. Gorgeous. What I'd always wanted. A yard for Peter to play in, fantastic trees everywhere, all green and moist underfoot. You need to have spent your life in California to appreciate those things."

"And you couldn't keep up the maintenance?"

She made a face. "You said it."

"As bad as that?"

"Yes." She stood up abruptly and said, "Coffee?"

"Please."

"Leaded or unleaded?"

Again, he remembered that from early American visits. "Leaded, please. The real stuff."

He wondered if that would be the end of the conversation; whether she felt willing or able to confide in him. And why on earth should she? Despite her reassurances that she remembered him well, she might only have been going through the motions. Just because he'd been carrying about the memory of a wonderful smile there was no reason to assume that he'd made any early impression on her.

She returned with freshly brewed coffee in hefty, oversized mugs. Clearly she had come to a decision, while in the kitchen. "We arrived here at the height of the property boom, bought the Redmond house, prepared to put down roots. When I tried to sell the market was flat, and I couldn't handle the mortgage. I mean, I couldn't even sell Pete's Porsche, what there was left of it, and the insurance is still dragging on because another guy was killed in the crash and they're counter-suing."

Ben stirred in a hefty spoonful of sugar. "But what about your parents? Or Pete's?"

"Wait. That was only the beginning. The tip of the iceberg. It turned out we'd been living way beyond our means ever since we married. I guess Pete was always working on expectations. I mean, he made good enough money, if we'd been careful. But we always lived like there was no tomorrow."

"And for him there was no tomorrow."

"Right."

It sounded horribly insensitive, once it had left his mouth. "Sorry. I didn't mean to be flippant about something so rotten."

She smiled slightly, but carefully avoided his eyes.

"That's okay. Being flippant's a darn sight better than crying all the time."

"And that's what you've been doing? It's been so rough?"

"Yes." She appeared to find the small pile of daisy petals more important at this moment than the coffee. "Everywhere I turned there were debts. Neither car had been paid for, one loan seemed to be paying off another. It was a crummy mess."

Ben felt immensely sorry for her but was unable to find any way to offer comfort, beyond offering a willing ear. "What did you do?"

She shrugged. "Humbled myself and asked my father-in-law for help."

"And?"

"So he paid off the outstanding debts. Left me solvent again. End of story."

"No, it's not," Ben persisted. It didn't explain why she came to be living with her son in, if not exactly squalor, at least straitened circumstances. She turned to look at him and he realized, perhaps for the first time, just how lovely her eyes were. Sort of shimmery green with gold flecks in them. Fine, dark lashes. One could get lost in those eyes.

"You're determined. Are you always a masochist? Do you want to hear the whole, sordid story?"

"Yes. Please."

She sighed. "The sticking point is Peter. Peter Sandford Pendleton the Third, may I remind you. In exchange for financial support they want me to hand him over to them, lock, stock and barrel. You need to have met my father-in-law to understand. He's every cartoonist's idea of the prototype self-made man. Having spoiled Pete rotten he really wanted to do the same with the only grandson. He couldn't believe his ears when I said 'thanks, but no thanks.' And that's where we're at right now."

Ben, vividly recalling the ghastly Pete, thought she should be awarded a medal for her bravery. It would have been awfully easy to capitulate, while still off balance from shock and grief. "Are you managing?"

"I work part-time. Three days a week. I made friends with a woman on this block, another single mother. She doesn't mind looking after Peter because it gives her some income. And he likes her, which is important to me."

Again she paused, and Ben, unable to find anything adequate to say, remained silent. Leigh refilled his mug.

"You know," she said, "This might sound dumb, but somehow having your back against the wall brings out the best in people. Nancy, she's the friend who cares for Peter, has been my life-line. We met when I moved here, about four months ago, and I feel I know her better than any of our rich, California friends. And I can rely on her, because she's been there before me. Can you understand that?"

Ben nodded. "The other sort are sometimes fair weather companions."

"Definitely."

He would have liked to pursue more of this conversation, but he was hesitant about rushing headlong in. She might consider him simply nosy. Instead he said, "Does Peter ever sleep over? Or could you find a baby sitter? I'd really like to take you out for a meal. Do you think that's possible?"

For the first time in the evening Leigh turned to him and smiled. It was not the thousand carat sort of his memory, but it was a great deal nearer to the delightful, sunny girl he remembered. "Ben, is this a date?"

He felt the red rising up his neck. Was he committing a

social blue, by suggesting that they go out? "Only if you want it to be. If not it's just an old friend offering you a free meal."

Her smile widened and a small spark kindled in her eyes. Why wasn't he aware of their beauty back in Frisco? Had he been blind?

"Thank you. I'd adore a real, honest-to-goodness date. And you don't know how happy I'll be to get out of this place, if only for one evening."

Inside him a small, fluttery sensation tightened his chest and made his breathing a touch irregular. Although, of course, it was nothing he couldn't control.

"That's great!" He hoped that the over-hearty tone was not too evident. "Then I'll pick you up at seven-thirty tomorrow."

Four

*S*o he had a date to organize. As his knowledge of
Seattle was minimal, Ben fell back on asking the chap
at the concierge desk where he might recommend to take
someone special, and booked a table. As he drove in the
rental car across the floating bridge which joined the city
with the east side of the lake, it occurred to him that he
should have asked Leigh to wear that red dress, the one he
remembered. Then he realized what a dope he was. How
many women held onto a dress for five years?

What would she have done with the kid? He hoped he
was already in bed, well out of sight. Even laying eyes on
that face, those big, dark eyes, made the hackles rise on the
back of his neck.

But he did better, this time, with the navigation; found

the apartment block first stab. It looked as depressingly shabby as on his previous visit.

■ ■ ■

Leigh, too, was feeling some of the excitement, although she was reluctant to admit it had anything to do with Ben. It was more, she told herself, the thrill of being invited out, being able to say a temporary farewell to the dreadful ordinariness of her present life.

"Where are we going?" She was delighted by the enormous box of candies Ben had produced. And impressed, despite herself, at how good looking he was, in that healthy, Antipodean way. Quite a hunk, Nancy would say. Worth laying. But Nancy, despite professing to being a total misogamist, saw every guy in terms of sex.

"I'm taking you to the Space Needle. I booked a table for eight o'clock. Okay, I hope? No hideous tales of food poisoning?"

"Fantastic! Pete . . ." It was on the tip of her tongue to say that her husband had often used the Space Needle for business meals, when she realized it might not be very tactful.

They circled the Seattle Center, a lasting monument to the Expo of the 'Sixties, and drew into the parking area. Ben handed the car keys over to a valet. Then they ascended in the elevator to the revolving restaurant atop the city's most distinguished landmark, and stepped out into another world.

It was early in the evening of a late summer's day, the sort which holds hints of the impending fall. The air was dramatic in its clarity. To the west the sun was slipping behind the purple range of the Olympics, creating an orange fringe of brilliance which spilled over onto the waters of Elliot Bay. The departing rays kissed the triangular snowcap of Mt. Rainier to the south and threw shadows across the wide stretch of tree and hill which reached towards the jagged skyline of the Cascades. The beauty of it all took Ben's breath away.

"I'm hopeless with words," he confessed as they sipped the champagne he ordered. "But if I were a poet I'd be suffering from writer's cramp right now, trying to get all this down on paper."

"It is pretty extraordinary." Leigh let her gaze wander over the city's darkening skyline. "And you don't sound inarticulate to me. Why do you put yourself down?"

"Oh, because I remember the sweat which used to break out on me every time I was faced with an essay at school. Talk about extracting blood! Gives me the shakes just thinking about it, even now, years on."

Leigh laughed. "And English was my easiest subject. Words sort of spilled out of me. But if I'd had my way I would have dropped everything that needed logical thought as soon as there were other options."

They both chose the wonderful local salmon, because Ben was determined to make this a date to remember. While they ate, the conversation remained light and rarely strayed into the realm of personal. Ben mentioned the flight program and related one or two minor anecdotes about Janna and Millie. Leigh told him of Peter's excitement at being allowed to sleep over for the first time ever with Nancy's Ryan.

He liked the thought that the apartment would be empty upon their return.

Over coffee he felt sufficiently confident to ask her how she imagined things would work out with the older

Pendletons. Leigh scrunched up her nose. It was a delightful gesture, and new to him.

"Compromise, I hope. You see, I do appreciate how they feel, because Pete was so special to them, and their only son at that. You'll understand better when you've a child of your own. They are part of Peter's family, whether I like it or not. The old man may be a dictator, but his wife, Do, is a doll. So I don't want to deprive them of all access to their grandson, or him to them. Maybe, one day he'll need them. And as for my mother, well." The wry expression said more than the lack of words.

"I was going to ask about your own family. From that face I gather your mother isn't exactly a tower of strength?"

Again she wrinkled her nose. It was an adorable little nose, with just a sprinkling of freckles. Like fairy dust, Ben's mother would say.

"You really are a masochist, aren't you. I noticed it the other day. Don't you find other people's history boring?"

"Not yours. And that's no answer, either. That's prevarication."

She laughed. "A five syllable word from a guy who flunked English? Not bad. And if you want to know about my family, here goes; but, remember, you asked for it." She began to speak rapidly, as if reciting from some old, often repeated catechism. "Father in the navy. Mother, how can I describe her? A bit of a snob. Parents divorced when I was five. Father never again contacts me. No birthday present, no Christmas card. Mother inherits money from decrepit aunt, moves from Frisco to Newport Beach. Has revolting little dog called Pookie, no kidding. And, at present, boyfriend, or gigolo, called Curtis."

"Hold it. Hold it." Ben intercepted. "My mind doesn't

think that fast. Go back to the start. Your father. Tell me about him."

Leigh remained silent while the waiter refilled her coffee. "I can't remember a lot about him. My memories are that he was fantastic, a very gentle man. I adored him. I think they fought a lot, but not noisy fights. Low arguments full of hissing, and icy silence. Then, one day he wasn't there. And I yearned for him." She gazed out across the skyline of the western mountains as they came slowly into view. "According to Mom he was playing around, although the words she used were more colorful. Couldn't keep his hands off the women. These days they'd charge him with sexual harassment."

Ben reached for the sugar and ripped the end off a small sachet. "And he just disappeared out of your life?"

"That's right. Like most kids I thought it must have been my fault; something I'd done which had driven him away. Perhaps I hadn't told him enough that I loved him. Mom was bitter and didn't care who knew it. She never remarried, but since she inherited Aunt Molly's money she allows herself the luxury of an escort. Calls him 'her young friend.' He's the slimiest thing on two legs."

Ben picked his words with care. "I appreciate that you value your independence, but couldn't she help you financially . . . er . . . until you're back on your feet?"

"Sure. And not even notice it. But she's never volunteered. And, come to that, I'd starve before I asked."

"Perhaps she thinks you're okay, financially. Or that the Pendleton parents are helping."

"Perhaps. Perhaps she's never bothered to find out, either."

Ben had a sudden, vivid picture of his own family. How deadly dull they seemed in comparison, and how wonderfully stable. Reliable. The Clan Beresford. What would happen to them, if one family member found himself to be in the straitened circumstances of Leigh? It was almost a rhetorical question. They'd be rallying round, digging into pockets.

"Do you see anything of your mother, then?"

"Not a lot. Not since Pete died, although she did grace us with her presence at the funeral. Curtis by her side, of course, to wipe away her tears and offer the necessary support. But at least no Pookie." She looked out across the lights of the city. "It's hard to explain my mom, without making her sound like someone from a horror movie, like 'Whatever Happened to Baby Alice?' That's her name, Alice. She really was quite a good mom, when I was little, but so bitter. I think she was dumped by another guy before she met my father, and she'd reached the conclusion that all men are bastards." She turned to Ben and smiled in a way that made his bones turn to jelly. "There are times when I believe she's right, of course."

He leapt to defend his gender. "Come off it! Not all of us. For heaven's sake . . ."

"I know you may appear different on the outside, but under the skin there's a touch of the same filthy lecher, waiting to pounce."

The specter of Pete clambering off that bed clad only in his shirt and socks rose before Ben's eyes. This was a dangerous path for the conversation to follow. "Go back to your mother. Tell me about Aunt Molly's money."

"Coward." When she laughed her eyes lit up and her face became so endearingly animated. "I think I'd rather fight."

"And I'd rather hear about your mother," Ben replied firmly, then added with less certainty, "That is, as long as you don't mind telling me?"

"No, I don't mind. You're a good listener. Where was I? Oh yes, wallowing in her assessment of men." Another sparkling, teasing glance at Ben. "After Daddy departed she needed to find work, and she had no marketable skills at all. So at first she worked in a bar, then she was a waitress. And she found it all pretty humiliating. She'd never imagined herself doing anything so lowly. Later she ran the restaurant, and being the manager was more her style. She liked throwing her weight around and having a bit of clout. At first we lived in this awful little dump in Oakland, then we moved out to the suburbs. I was about ten, I guess."

"No more kids?" Ben interrupted.

"No. Just me. I went to Berkeley, met Pete at a party, married him. Then, about three years ago, she inherited all this money. Aunt Molly was my mom's great aunt, and so ancient I think we'd all forgotten about her. She'd been a recluse for years, living in some great old estate up on the Hudson. That's all."

"No, it's not. Doesn't your mother believe in sharing?"

Leigh's smile was wry. "Not this, even if I humbled myself to ask her. This she sees as her just reward for all those years of having to live that other life. She sold the mansion on the Hudson for bundles, bought herself a place in Newport Beach, amongst 'folks with whom she's comfortable,' allows Curtis to wait on her like a slave and lavishes affection on Pookie like there's no tomorrow."

"What about her grandson?"

Again Leigh's expression spoke volumes. "Wouldn't you think she'd love him to death? But, I guess, she's too involved with her own life, or something. Bridge parties and Charity evenings. But she does send him fabulous presents. Guess what he had for his second birthday? A complete set of the Encyclopedia Britannica. I kid you not. Not the junior edition. The whole caboodle!"

He raised his shoulders slightly. "So? She wants her grandson to become a Nobel prize winner." Again he returned to the current train of his thoughts. "Have you considered living with her, or is that a daft idea?"

"Forget it. Allow a three year old to sully her precious place? Not to mention the dog. I forgot to say that Pookie is very highly strung. Some might think neurotic."

She put out her hand to emphasize her point, and Ben seized the opportunity to grasp it. It was very attractive; small, fine boned. This, he realized, was their first ever physical contact.

He wasn't sure, however, that Leigh appreciated the significance of the moment, because she continued almost without a pause. "I know what you're getting at. You want to find some way of shepherding me out of that miserable apartment, and I do appreciate that, Ben. You see yourself as some sort of knight in shining armor. But forget it. Things will work out for Peter and me. We'll manage, in our own time, in our own way. We're survivors. And asking my mother for financial aid is simply a no-no."

"But . . ."

"No buts. That's just the way it is."

Five

heir departure from the Space Needle coincided with a crowd of sports fans emerging from the stadium, and the approach roads to the freeway were jammed. Ben didn't mind. Anything which prolonged the evening met with favor in his eyes.

"This place reminds me a lot of Sydney, you know." He inched the car along Denny Way. "Of course, the trees are different. Ours are mostly gums. But the way the city stretches to the water. You've never been to Sydney?"

Leigh watched the cars that crawled past as they approached the ramp. "I've never been further than Mexico."

"Well, you ought to go. It's a fantastic city, though I say so in all modesty. I've my own place. It's the top half of a house that's about ninety years old, and it has a view of the harbor you wouldn't believe."

"I've seen pictures, of the bridge and the Opera House. And those koalas the airline uses for advertising. They're cute."

In the glow cast by the headlights of creeping vehicles Ben grinned down at her. "Don't mention them. They're the ads of our rivals. Deadly enemies."

"Sorry!"

Such contrition seemed a very sensible excuse to reach over and take her hand.

"How's the flying going?" Leigh asked presently. She had not withdrawn her hand.

"Reasonably. We spent today out at Moses Lake, doing touch and goes."

"Touch and goes? That sounds like a kids' game."

"Not this sort." Ben reluctantly released her fingers as he negotiated the entry onto the freeway and allowed the car to gather speed. "We fly in, just touch the wheels down, then climb, circle, touch down again."

"It makes me feel giddy even thinking of it. When do you go home to Australia?"

"Here's your hat . . . what's the hurry, eh?" His expression was quizzical. "And I was imagining you'd had a good time."

"I have. It was a fantastic meal. And you may not have kissed the Blarney Stone, Ben Beresford, but you're a wonderful listener. You know, I can't recall telling anybody, apart from Nancy, half of what I told you tonight."

"Even we dumb types have our uses." He felt, rather than saw, her smile in the gloom. "The only project I have to work on now is your poor opinion of men."

"Don't even try," Leigh said in a small voice. "That's cast in stone."

41

"Crikey! You are a case."

They drove in easy silence for some while, across the long, low platform of the bridge, turning off the freeway to take the road which followed the eastern shore of Lake Washington. The glorious sunset had been supplanted by a cloudless, starry sky from which a discus moon touched everything with a sheen of silver.

Ben pulled the car to a halt alongside a small, lakeside park and switched off the engine. "Can I tell you something, Leigh? You probably won't even recall the moment, but you made one almighty impression on me that first evening we met. Remember? Your engagement party. I thought I'd never seen anyone with a smile half as fantastic as yours. And that impression has stayed with me, all these years." He rested one arm on the wheel and half turned to her. "Sort of like a yardstick, against which I've measured other girls. I'd think to myself, 'Does she have a smile like Leigh's? Does it affect me in the same way hers did, that night?' You were so . . . so . . . happy. You radiated joy, and it was like a fire which warmed everybody who was near. And there was jasmine in flower, on the balcony. Ever since that night I've only to smell jasmine and I think of a smashing girl in a red dress and a halo of happiness. And Leigh, she's gone, that girl. I know that she's lost her husband, but she's also lost a great deal more."

Leigh, sitting very still and thinking that for a guy who professed to be a dunce with words he was doing pretty well, spoke very quietly. "Life's like that, Ben. I believe it's called growing up."

"The hell with that! I don't know how to put this tactfully, but are you still missing him? Missing Pete? Is that the only reason why you've changed?"

Her voice even quieter, Leigh replied, "Not entirely."

"Then let me help. I'd do anything to bring that happy person back. Honestly. Anything."

"You're remembering somebody who's no longer there," Leigh objected. "Like a school photo which you tucked away in your wallet, and every now and then take out. You said it yourself, I'm no longer that girl. I've moved on from there. I'm a mother and a widow. A poor widow, at that. Practically a welfare case."

"But you know that's not important to me. Listen. I've got another week or so here, if all goes well. We could go out some more, have some fun. You must know the right sort of places." His voice trailed away. He wasn't too sure whether he was putting across all that he wanted to say with any degree of success.

Leigh looked away from him, across the stretch of platinum water, towards the skyline of Seattle. "Are you trying to say you've . . ." The phrase, 'got the hots for me' sounded crude in her ears, and unworthy of the moment.

Ben almost read her mind. "Yes."

She turned fully towards him, aware of the angles and crags of his face as the moonlight played on them, of the shadows which hid his eyes. "Ben . . . don't."

"Don't what?"

"Don't fall for me. I'm the wrong person. You've done so much for my confidence, just taking me out tonight, telling me that. And you're a great guy. In another life I'd have fallen for you like a shot. But as it is, I don't think I'll ever let myself get into a serious relationship again."

Hurting for her, longing to touch her again, Ben traced the silhouette of her cheek with one gentle finger. "Leigh, you're crying! Don't cry. Please."

"I can't help it. I don't like disappointing you. You've been so kind."

"Then, if you think that, let me help." He was starting to sound like the message on an answering machine.

"I can't. I can't take the risk."

He wanted to pull her across the seat and comfort her with a hug. Why did this bloody car have bucket seats? "Why? What are you frightened of?"

Her voice was no more than a whisper. "When it all starts to crumble. I won't be able to bear the pain."

■ ■ ■

The light was on in Leigh's apartment, when presently they pulled up before it.

"Trouble?" Ben queried.

"I don't know. But it can't be much, because I let Nancy know where we were. She would've called."

Her friend let them in while Leigh was still fumbling for her key. She was a tough, skinny woman, all points and angles. Probably only in her thirties, by Ben's estimation, but well worn.

"Hi, kids. Good food?"

"Fantastic. What's up, Nance?"

She shrugged. "Poor old Peter had a fit of homesickness. Missed his own bed, so I brought 'em both over here and tucked them in. Ryan's in your bed." Ryan was Nancy's four year old son.

Leigh said, "Coffee?" and disappeared into the kitchen.

"So. You had a good time?" Nancy asked cheerfully. She was very impressed by Ben. According to Leigh she was simply accepting a free dinner from the brother of one of Pete's old golfing mates. No mention of a hunk, no mention of thick, sun bleached hair that fell casually across a wide brow, or the bluest of eyes. No casual reference to the length of thigh and tightest little butt ever to grace a pair of pants. Quite a dark horse, old Leigh.

Ben could have screamed with frustration. Not of the sexual variety, because he'd never exactly envisaged them between the sheets; but he was not prepared to let the night end without having extracted another date from Leigh. This sheila's presence put a real kibosh on the evening. Trust bloody Peter to sabotage him.

However, aware that Nancy was important to Leigh, he made rather stilted conversation until the coffee arrived, drank his in gulps which would have made a lesser man quail and stood to take his leave. It was abundantly apparent that Nancy had no intention of making herself scarce. Leigh saw him to the door, which opened directly from the living room onto the passage way. The smell of cat pee rose to meet them.

"Bye, Ben. Great meeting you," Nancy called loudly.

He drew Leigh out into the passage, pinioning her against the wall with a hand on either side of her shoulders. He could still make out the fine, silvery lines where her tears had trickled down her cheeks. He kept his voice low, aware that Nancy's ears were probably flapping in her anxiety to hear. "Listen. I'm not leaving until you promise to see me again."

"Ben . . ."

"Ben nothing."

"I can't . . . Peter . . ."

"Peter fiddle. We'll take him with us. How about a picnic? Sunday's free. We're not flying, and I'll still have the car. Is that okay with you?"

Leigh kept her eyes lowered, reluctant to meet his.

"I guess . . . but . . ."

"Then that's settled. Ten o'clock, and my treat. I'll have the hotel fix us a boxed lunch."

He raised her chin with one hand, forcing her to meet his gaze. His voice was even lower. "You know, there really is Life after Pete. Give me a chance, Leigh."

He kissed her, no more than a butterfly kiss which brushed her lips, and was gone.

Six

ecause Ben was providing transport and provisions, Leigh was in charge of destination for the picnic. She chose to take them all to Deception Pass.

Nancy thought she was a fool, even contemplating another outing with Ben, and told her so.

"That's easy to say, harder to do," Leigh replied, gathering together a change of clothing for Peter. "You've not come up against his determination. He rode roughshod over everything I said. I think he'd have kidnapped me, if I'd refused to see him again."

"He's too good looking, and too sexy. You're playing with fire. And remember what Mommy taught you: people who play with fire get their fingers burned."

Leigh sighed. "I hear you, hon. But you have to admit

he's balm to a pretty battered ego. And another thing, Nance, he's such a good listener. He actually hears what I'm saying. I'm not used to that."

"Except when you tell him you're not in the market, let alone interested in another relationship."

Another sigh. "Except that."

■ ■ ■

Sunday was made in heaven. Clear blue skies, a stillness in the air, splashes of autumn colors in the broad leafed trees which lined the north-bound inter-state highway. A friendly, warm September. They turned off the freeway, following the road which wound south through cedar and hemlock stands towards the tip of Whidbey Island.

Ben was immensely impressed by Deception Pass, as Leigh hoped he would be. One minute they were amongst darkly towering conifers, the next the iron arches of the two bridges which linked Whidbey with the mainland came into view. There, far below, the amazingly aquamarine tidal flow swirled and eddied through steep, narrow walls of rock in its rush to escape Puget Sound and join the waters of the Straits. And out to sea could be seen the soft bulk of Vancouver Island and towering peaks of the Olympics.

They lugged their picnic down the path and onto the log-strewn beach. Actually, Ben did the lugging while Peter clung to his mother's hand.

Peter had been surprisingly awkward about the whole notion of a picnic. Leigh assumed he would leap at the idea, but he needed coaxing into the car, insisted that she sit in the back beside him and refused to say more than a gruff 'hi' to Ben. Even when Ben produced a small candy bar by way of a peace offering, Peter simply eyed it and buried his face in his mother's skirt. He always was a little uncomfortable with men, and more so since his father's death, but that wasn't the whole story. For some reason he'd taken a dislike to Ben, which was difficult to fathom. According to Nancy he sensed that Ben might be a rival, and resented it. But that answer was too flip to please Leigh.

Be that as it may, he was giving a pretty fair impression of being bonded to her with super-glue, refusing any help but hers, addressing his every utterance her way, and scowling darkly at Ben. And, once his small offering had been scorned, Ben did not go any further out of his way to win Peter's approval.

It was easier after they'd eaten the delicious boxed lunch prepared by the hotel. Leigh was reminded of a remark once heard and stored away. 'Men are simple creatures: slaves to their stomachs and their wedding tools. Satisfy both of those and they'll be yours for life.' She wondered which hunger her mother had failed to satisfy in her father? Which one, come to that, she herself had failed to nourish in Pete, however hard she tried.

They ate deviled eggs and chicken drumsticks, fresh fruit and a crusty French baguette, all of it washed down with a very good Washington State wine. There was a can of pop for Peter. Even entertainment was provided while they ate. Two harbor seals lolled in the waves near the beach; boot-button eyes brightly regarding the poor, shore-stranded creatures with as much curiosity as the humans were watching them.

Once they were finished Ben stretched out on a reach of clear sand with his hands behind his head and gazed, contented, at the cloudless arc of the sky. "I thought it always rained in Seattle," he remarked. "I've been here nearly two weeks and there's not been as much as one sprinkling."

"That's a rumor which is circulated to stop too many people moving up here. But it does rain, that's for sure. There are times in the winter when you wonder if it'll ever stop."

Peter was unpacking several small cars from the bag which Leigh had furnished for him. He found a convenient spot and began creating roads and tunnels from the storm-tossed driftwood which littered the beach. He became quickly absorbed in his play. Roads and cars held an abiding fascination for him. It was very peaceful.

Ben squinted into the distance. "Those birds; the big ones, circling. Are they eagles?"

Leigh followed his gaze, shielding her eyes from the dazzle of sun off water. "Yes, bald eagles. You can see their white heads and tail feathers. They winter over here by the hundreds, but most return north for the summer. We're lucky to see any at this time of year."

Ben's voice was lazy. "I'm always lucky. That's me. Lucky Ben."

He reached an idle hand across, grabbed her by the wrist and pulled her towards him. Caught off balance Leigh toppled, laughing and protesting, onto his chest. He held her there, smiling into her eyes, their faces inches apart. She smelled of some sweet, unnamed fragrance. He could have kissed her, so easily.

Peter broke their moment. "Let my Mommy go!" He leaped to the defense of his mother. "Let her go! You're a bad man."

"It's okay, Punkin," Leigh reassured him, "We're only playing. Ben's just teasing me, having fun." But Peter had to sit on her knee and be cuddled for some minutes to be totally sure. When, happy that Ben was not again about to threaten her, he returned a bit hesitantly to his cars,

Leigh turned to Ben. "Let me see your hand."

"Why?"

She took the hand he proffered and examined it. "Not my imagination. I thought I felt them. These two fingers are callused. What does a pilot do to create calluses like these?"

"Not a lot," Ben replied lazily, enjoying having his hand held and examined. "But sailors do quite a bit of hauling on sheets, and we all sail, we Beresfords. My father keeps his boat at the Yacht Squadron, just across the bay from where I live, and most weeks at least one of us'll take her out. We all sailed as boys." He shaded his eyes to see her better. "You have to imagine it, Leigh. Sydney Harbor on a warm summer's evening. It's beaut. As lovely, in its way, as this place. There'll be hundreds of craft out, racing or just cruising, with their sails looking like a storm of butterflies. I wish you'd come down, sometime, spend a few weeks in Australia, and I could show you."

"And pigs might fly. I have a hard enough time scraping together enough to pay the rent and keep Peter in shoes. The only time I'll get to anywhere further away than Seattle is when I win the lottery. And that's never, because I can't afford to play."

Which brought them, tidily, to another topic he was hoping to discuss. "About your in-laws. I've been thinking . . ."

"Mmm?" Leigh was distracted. Her son had discovered the half-buried debris of earlier, less punctilious picnickers. "Punkin, don't touch that. That's somebody else's trash."

"You're right, about them," Ben continued, "About not shutting them out entirely. I tried to picture my parents, if their grandchildren were just whisked away for ever. It'd kill my mother. Ditto the Pendletons, I reckon."

"Oh, them." She was listening with only half an ear.

"Yes. Well, I heard from their attorney, yesterday. It appears that they may accept my compromise."

"Which is?"

"Peter stays with me. I have sole custody. They can see him whenever they want to, with me in tow at present, while he's still young; on his own when he's old enough. A bit like visitation rights."

"Sounds sensible. And in exchange?"

Leigh made a face. "Who knows? That's still in the pipeline, awaiting their counter-offer. Some sort of child maintenance which would enable us to live someplace that's not a health hazard? Do you think that sounds as if I'm greedy?"

Ben glanced at Peter, saw he had his back to them and was absorbed in his game again, and made a lunge for Leigh. He pulled her down against him and gave her a quick, hard kiss before releasing her. She sat up like a disengaged bedspring.

"My darling girl." He laughed at the speed of her recoil, the sudden color which sprang into her cheeks. "It sounds extremely sensible. As sensible a solution as I'd expect from a gutsy, independent person like you."

"Thanks for your approval." She started to pack away their picnic goods in a bustling, busy way. "And I am not your darling girl."

"Oh no?" Ben, grinned at her in a way which she found even more unsettling than his stolen kiss. "Just give me the opportunity to prove you wrong."

Seven

They drove homeward down the length of Whidbey,
the island lying sleepy and mellow in the afternoon
sun. They walked and explored, stopped for ice creams and
drove off the main highway to investigate several small and
delightful townships.

The length of the wait for the ferry which would carry
them across Puget Sound was a bit daunting, but Peter fell
asleep and that helped. It would have been a good time for
Ben to follow up several strains of thought which required
pursuing, but Leigh, he recognized, had withdrawn slightly
since lunch. He didn't want to sabotage all the progress
which he felt he'd made during the day. So he contented
himself with conversation of the non-investigative variety,
and took pleasure in watching her.

"Come in," Leigh said briefly when, some time later, they reached her apartment. "Do you want to stay for a bite?"

"Do you want to have me?"

Leigh was carrying a sleepy, sticky Peter, his arms around her neck, his face scrunched against her shoulder. Over his head she replied a bit briskly, "Sure. On my terms." She had spent some of that time while waiting for the ferry in thought, as well.

Ben grinned. "And what are they?"

"No sudden lunges. No catching me unaware."

"You're a spoilsport!"

"Yes, that's me. But don't say you weren't warned. And you'll have to wait while I bathe Peter."

"Okay." Ben capitulated. "You win. Hands-off-Ben, that's me."

She made them tuna sandwiches in the tiny kitchen. They ate them on their knees and watched a comedy on the television. It was very relaxing, happily domestic. When the comedy ended Leigh brewed coffee.

Ben said cautiously, "Leigh, . . . Pete . . . was he a good father? Supportive and that?"

She knelt on the floor beside the low table. "Are we into compulsory confession time already?"

"No compulsion. Only if you want. As you know, I'm putty in your hands."

She poured the coffee and handed him the sugar. "Why do you ask?"

"Something you said the other day. It rang a bell."

Leigh didn't look at him. She held the mug between her palms and gazed into some other world. "Not particularly. He loved Punkin, of course, but he had no idea of parenthood and was very inconsistent with him."

"In what way?"

"One minute nothing was good enough for his son; the next he was brushing him off as a total nuisance. And it goes without saying that he expected him to be an all-star athlete, like himself." She shifted uncomfortably, still averting her eyes.

"Does it bother you to talk about it?" Ben asked, noticing that involuntary movement. "I said there was no compulsion."

"It's okay. Really. For some reason you seem to have cast yourself in the role of my Father Confessor, though I can't imagine why."

He grinned. "Then you're being dense. Only give me the chance and I'll show you other facets of my brilliant personality. Not to mention my remarkable physical attributes."

"Now you're bragging. And being crude."

Ben, sitting on the sofa, patted the vacant space by his side. "Come and sit here. I promise I've got no ulterior motive and my principles are exemplary. It just seems to me that you could do with a friend. And why not me? Brother Ben, friend to the poor and needy."

It was a tempting offer. "Hands off? You promise?"

"Cross my heart. My hands won't stray as much as one inch."

She sat on the sofa, leaving a decent space between them, but Ben drew her close until his arm was round her and her head was nestled against his shoulder. It was a very convenient height, his shoulder.

"Nancy says that when you unburden your soul to someone you're giving that person power over you."

Ben was beginning to hate Nancy. "What utter tripe!"

"What do you want to know?"

"Anything. What you want to tell me. To talk about."

The pause seemed to stretch towards eternity. "I suppose what Pete wanted was a son who was just like him. A tremendous sportsman, and brilliant too. He had this great idea we should use those educational flash cards from the moment of birth. Have you seen them? Have they reached Australia?"

"Yes. Jane says they probably send more kids to the funny farm than any other single cause. Stressed out infants. She's a pediatrician, you know." He paused for some more coffee. "So the proud papa stands poised beside the delivery table . . . ?"

"You don't imagine Pete was in the delivery room, do you? He'd faint at the sight of a scratch. Not 'we.' Me. I was to devote myself to raising the genius child. It was a fantastic idea, in Pete's mind. I would be kept happily occupied, his son would benefit by becoming a world-beater. He'd win, both ways."

Comfortable against Ben's shoulder, his arm warmly round her, Leigh closed her eyes and allowed herself to be transported back to those earlier times. Already they were losing a third dimension, taking on the aspects of flat snapshots in her memory. She could remember the moments after the birth, when Pete had walked into her room, flowers in hand, looking for all the world like a Cheshire cat. He bent to kiss her, to congratulate her upon having done as ordered, and presented him with an heir: and she smelled the elusive aroma of Persuasion clinging to him.

His current girlfriend was lavish in her use of Persuasion. It had been on the tip of Leigh's tongue to say tartly that perhaps Donna might be a bit more discreet in her choice of perfume, but she'd bitten it back. The birth had been long and she was feeling dog-tired. She hadn't the energy to initiate a fight, not then, and, anyway, she'd learned through bitter experience that the only person hurt on such occasions was herself. Angry confrontations, deeply damaging to her, just bounced off Pete.

She didn't tell Ben any of that, because it was still too humiliating to relate. The one person with whom she'd shared such revelations was Nancy, because her marriage had not been ideal either. The thing which added extra spice to Nancy's was her ex-husband's habit of using her as a punching bag.

Instead she told Ben about Pete's insistence that his son be toughened up. How this translated into not picking him up when he was distressed, but leaving him to cry it out. How this behavior had wrung her heart, so that she'd crept into the bedroom to feed and comfort the baby. The bitter arguments this would cause, because Pete was sure that his way was the only way, and, besides, he didn't like to be crossed. Then there were the occasions when he considered his son old enough to take a serious interest in ball-related activities.

"His father boasted that Pete could catch and hit a ball when he was two. Most kids aren't coordinated enough at that age, and I'm sure the old man exaggerated a bit anyway, over the years, as proud parents will. But Pete would take Punkin out into the yard and toss balls at him. Of course, the sessions would end disastrously, the baby would be in tears and Pete would accuse me of making a sissy out of him. In his eyes to be a sissy was the ultimate sin."

When she ran out of narrative they sat very still in the dim light of the single lamp. Leigh, because she felt more comfortable than she had in years; Ben, because he was at a complete loss for words. He was choked up with such fury that it was like a thorn bush sticking in his throat. And, curiously, although quite a lot of the rage was directed at himself, even more was being pointed in Leigh's direction. His every instinct had been correct, all those years ago. He shouldn't have punched the skunk. He should have strangled him, then and there, and saved everybody a great deal of trouble.

But Leigh was to blame, too. How could she have chosen so badly? But presently the lump dissolved in his throat and he was able to say quietly, "Thank you, Leigh. Thank you for telling me."

"You're a good listener. I said so before. You've missed your vocation. You should have gone into the church."

He twisted his head to squint down at her. "Father Benjamin? The celibate life? You're kidding."

Leigh giggled. It was a sound that warmed his heart. "No, perhaps not."

He glanced at his watch. It was nearly midnight. "We're flying tomorrow, early. I've got to make a move. That is, assuming I'm not being invited to spend the night here?"

"Absolutely not."

He sighed, a heavy, theatrical sigh. "My darling, you don't know what you're missing."

"I can imagine. And thanks, but no thanks."

"No second chances? But did I gain honor marks for good behavior?" He took her silence to indicate agreement. "Then at least I deserve a reward for that."

He turned her head with his free hand and kissed her with considerable expertise and a great deal of feeling, holding her close to him.

Leigh felt herself melting, as though the shape of her body were fusing against his, curve finding hollow the length of their torsos. Somewhere, deep inside her, she was aware of a flame kindling and flickering. She wrenched herself back like one bitten.

Her mother had said, "They do that, men. They're full of animal lust, and they'll use your need for love to sabotage you. That's all it is, with them. No commitment at all. Animal lust. Rutting. And then, just as you become fond of them, bingo! Off to the next conquest. It's a sort of sport to them. And then they swap dirty tales about you in the locker room."

"It's been a lovely day, Ben," she said, a little awkwardly. He looked like a kid who just discovered that the Tooth Fairy was really his mom. "Thanks for the picnic, and everything."

He grinned and ruffled his hair in a schoolboy gesture. Then he stood up, stretching his legs. "Yeah, well, I enjoyed it, too." He paused while he searched for the right approach. "Leigh?"

"What?"

"There's a Delivery Banquet coming up; on Wednesday, at the Columbus Club. That's when the keys of the plane are officially handed over, and it becomes ours. I can bring a guest, and I want to take you. Will you come?"

He saw her hesitate, stiffen.

"Please?" His voice was pleading. "After that I'll be out of your hair. On the other side of the Pacific. Do you think that'll be far enough away?"

Leigh wasn't sure whether anywhere would be far enough away for her peace of mind. And yet, one dinner, at the Columbus Club . . .

"Maybe," she said. "But I am not your darling."

Eight

"*Y*ou've got a screw loose," Nancy exclaimed. "You're bananas. Stark raving mad. How can you contemplate going out with the guy again? That's not playing with fire, it's juggling dynamite."

They were in Nancy's apartment, which was a carbon copy of Leigh's. It was a gray, drizzly day, almost certainly conjured up by the weather gods to counter Ben's unbalanced introduction to Washington weather. Leigh assumed that they still flew, despite inclement conditions.

The small boys, confined to indoors, were playing with building blocks which littered the living room floor. Nancy was preparing food for them all. The kitchen was pungent with the spices and seasonings of her favorite chili. Leigh sat on an elderly bar stool with her back awkwardly against the edge of one cupboard.

"Mmm. I know all that."

"Then, why on earth . . . ?"

"We're going to the Columbus Club. Some sort of official occasion, which he called a Delivery Banquet. Evidently the airline is handed the keys to the new plane. You know, Nance, I never realized they switched on the engines of a plane like a car. Or do you think it's just symbolic?"

Nancy had no idea, and no interest. She was much more concerned with the mental health of her friend. In her view, one failed marriage and two disastrous liaisons down the road, mental health was dependent upon keeping guys, all guys, at arm's length. Having seen Ben she could, of course, appreciate why Leigh found him hard to resist. Which was all the more reason why, as a stalwart friend, she should apply herself to injecting some steel into the younger woman's backbone.

She saw the situation as a bit like an Emotional Addicts Anonymous, in which it was one's duty to leap to the support of any fellow addict who found her defenses crumbling. "So it's a fancy party?"

"I guess. The Columbus is about the smartest place in town. Pete thought so, anyway. He applied to become a member the minute we set foot in Seattle."

"You telling me you're a member?" Nancy put her head to one side, enquiringly.

"No. His application was still in the pipeline, at the time of the accident. Anyway, can you imagine me finding membership fees, right now?"

Behind them, in the living room, a minor squabble broke out as two small boys sought possession of the same building block. Nancy called briskly, "Cut it out, you guys!"

There had been no opportunity in Nancy's life for much education. Experience, she would say, was her teacher, and her classroom was the School of Hard Knocks.

"Then the next day he flies home. To Australia." Leigh wanted Nancy to justify her decision. "So I can't come to much harm, can I? I mean, what can happen at a formal dinner, in the middle of a bunch of people?"

Nancy thought while she opened a pack of chicken franks for the two small boys. "Look at things this way, kid: ask yourself, why do we fall for guys? The answer's biology, isn't it. Hormones and human nature. Okay, let's agree, we all enjoy doing it. We were made that way, so that the human race would carry on. Nothing to do with our heads. All hormones, dictating our actions. It's the pay-off that hurts. Because, having lured you by your biological needs, this bastard then proceeds to tie you down, hold you as a prisoner. And all because you thought you'd enjoy a romp in the hay."

"You sound just like my mother. Apart from the dirty language."

"Then your Mom's a sensible gal. Believe me, I've been there ahead of you. And her, too."

"But I don't like sex," Leigh objected. She opened the bag of rolls which Nancy tossed to her. "Nobody could ever catch me that way. It was awful with Pete, because he always seemed to be having a good time, and I was, what's the phrase? 'Wondering if we shouldn't paint the bedroom ceiling.' I gritted my teeth until the whole business was over. It certainly wasn't fun." She took out two rolls and opened them. "And anyway, as I told you, Ben's going back to Australia. I'll never see him again."

"And taking a chunk of you with him? Holding you hostage?"

Leigh's voice was quiet. "No, not really. I'm still all in one piece, I think."

Nancy jammed the chicken franks between the bread, was liberal with the ketchup and called briskly, "Kids, move your fannies up to that table! Grub's up." Over her shoulder she spoke to Leigh. "You see? There's more than one way to skin a cat. He probably realized you don't like sex. So he tried another approach."

She was right, Leigh thought. She jumped like a startled jack rabbit whenever Ben as much as touched her. He must have noticed. He certainly had noticed. Was his kindness motivated exclusively by his desire to get her between the sheets? She knew her mother would say so. But, in that case, he must be one darned good actor.

She picked up their two bowls and followed Nancy to the table. The chili was delicious, just the right amount of bite. She did wish Ryan would not chew so noisily, or at least be encouraged to close his mouth. Nancy was not too hot on table manners, happy enough when the food ended up inside her son, rather than on the floor.

"Will you baby-sit for me on Wednesday, Nance? You can put Ryan down in my bed again."

"For you, kid, anything. Just don't say I didn't warn you when you find that you've fallen for this guy hook, line and sinker."

"I won't. Promise."

No need to say to Nancy that perhaps it was like bolting the barn door after the horse had run away, and that probably the damage was done already.

It was a blessing that Ben would be on his way home, Thursday.

Nine

$\mathcal{B}$en was by nature not particularly introverted. Searching for the deeper meaning of things was quite out of character. Nor did he seek the motivation behind his every action. However, he did not need to be an Einstein to gauge that the Delivery Banquet stood a very good chance of being Date of the Year. Which was lucky, to say the least. He had reached the stage when it was very important to offer Leigh a good time, not to mention his desire to impress her.

His nature was not vain, but to say that how he looked was unimportant was to simplify the matter. If the face which stared back at him from the mirror each morning were hideous to contemplate, the body below it miserable and puny, his character would probably have formed differently, in order to accommodate those different facts.

As it was, he was born the third son of a family remarkable for its above average looks. He was blessed by nature with the twin advantages of build and coordination, and topped by the family's trademark, that thatch of flaxen hair which was so striking. Also characteristic of the family, the fairness did not extend to eyebrows and lashes.

Because the alliteration was catchy they were from earliest days the Beresford Boys. Once Ben was beyond the 'tag-along' stage they traveled in a pod. Their interests were similar, their ages spread over only five years. People, seeing them, confused them. Perhaps John was tallest by an inch, and certainly Ben was the fairest. David was the most scholarly, but externally that was hard to see. Few people, during their growing up years, bothered to sort out which was which. In the neighborhood, much of school and the Yacht Squadron, they were simply the Beresford Boys.

It was an official occasion, so Ben wore his uniform to the banquet. Again, nothing particularly unusual in that to him. All schoolchildren in Australia wear school uniforms to some degree, so it was no great shakes; only his years at the University of Sydney separated school's and pilot's official garb. But he thought it was to his advantage that Leigh see him thus kitted out. It was common knowledge that women were dippy about guys in uniform, a syndrome well documented from the years of war. And even these days blokes in the Armed Services were notoriously successful with women.

He had another small item in his arsenal: some jasmine for Leigh, which seemed totally appropriate. Its flowers might be rather insignificant alongside showier blooms, but its perfume was as much Leigh to him as was the memory of her famous smile.

Thus equipped he drove across the floating bridge to collect her.

■ ■ ■

Leigh was thoroughly uncomfortable about the dinner, in particular, and Ben in general. The last forty-eight hours had not brought reassurance. In fact, after listening to all than Nancy had to say, she was poised on the verge of full-flowering panic. Nancy was, of course, right. She was allowing Ben to manipulate her into a situation that was totally against her better judgment. He would be skipping off tomorrow and taking a piece of her with him. Accompanying him to this dinner was offering herself to further heartbreak.

And then, what about an appropriate dress? She owned several suitable for such an evening, all of them were legacies from Life with Pete, but most were packed away and inaccessible. Space in the apartment was so limited she'd brought only everyday pants and skirts to it. And buying something new was out of the question.

In the end she rifled through a suitcase of heavily creased articles and found the dress which she'd bought, originally, for her engagement party. She adored it at the time, and subsequently wore it almost to death. A dress which didn't protest that in the intervening years she'd filled out a bit and which had fortunately withstood the march of fashion, too. She'd always loved the way the skirt, cut on the bias, floated and swirled round her legs. The color was such a clear red without a hint of blue or yellow in it. That was pretty special, as well.

Was Nancy right? Not in her assertion that men trapped women into servitude by way of their sexual appetites. Leigh thought that any desire she might once have possessed was well and truly killed off by Pete. But was Ben deliberately presenting himself in the role of willing ear, as a way to make himself indispensable? It sounded so devious, when you thought of it in that way. Ben didn't come across as deceitful. But then, he was always referring to how inarticulate he was, when clearly that wasn't the case. Another deception, to set her at ease?

Nancy talked about keeping up your defenses, remembering that all men were tomcats at heart. She reminded her to allow no amorous little diversions in which he could work his sexual magic, to be sure that the conversation stay vague and general.

She kept it up until the moment that Ben rang the outside bell and Leigh said over the intercom, "Wait downstairs, Ben. I'll be right with you."

She descended the flight of dismal cement steps, and there he was, standing in the lobby. He held his peaked cap in one hand, a corsage of flowers in the other. The dim light of the street lamp, on this prematurely dark, damp evening, gleamed like old silver on his hair, and her heart sank.

Ben's voice was warm with pleasure. "You're wearing that dress!"

She hoped that her tone hid the dismay she was feeling. "Hi. Yes. I hope you don't mind. I mean, it's appropriate for this evening, isn't it?"

"I'd thought about asking you to wear it, if you still had it. You look fantastic. Can I give you a kiss?" But he was teasing. His expression was devoid of anything threatening.

"No!"

"Can I call you 'my darling?'"

But she didn't rise to that bait, either.

As they drove back towards the Columbus Club and

the city he said, in face of her rather strained silence, "What's up?"

"Nothing," Leigh lied. "I had rather a rough day at work."

How could she explain about her father, the gentle, handsome father who was in the Navy; and who wore a uniform, too? How could she say, 'Daddy and uniforms are intertwined in my mind like stitches in a patchwork quilt, and when I saw you standing there I was suddenly five again, and he was coming back from a tour at sea, with a present for me? And I was running downstairs to welcome him home. Until suddenly he wasn't coming home ever again. And there were no more presents, either.'

How could she express the ache inside her which that void had caused? Describe how tender was the scar tissue which covered it? Trying, with only limited success, to bury those suddenly sharp and painful memories, she gave herself a mental shake. This was not the way to begin an evening, a very special evening. And surely she deserved the chance to create some happy memories?

"I never did remember to ask you about your work," Ben said. "Tell me what you do."

Leigh moved gratefully into neutral territory. "My degree is in Special Ed. There's a school for young adults, not far down the hill from the apartment complex. Mostly kids who've suffered head injuries. I work there, two-and-a-half days a week. They would have me for more, but I don't want to leave Peter any longer than I do already."

Working with brain-damaged young adults for half-a-day would, in Ben's limited experience, be enough to throw one into a fit of the dismals for a week. It explained why she was acting a bit miserably, this evening. In the face of her silence he kept up a flow of cheerful nothings, the sort which require no answer, but babble gently away until they merge into a stream of words and sentences. This was their last evening together, at least for the foreseeable future, and nothing, absolutely nothing, was going to be allowed to ruin it.

The Columbus Club was housed in the tallest tower in the city. It was a pity that the evening was so dreary, because the most spectacular views in the entire area were those from the club. But even the dampness could not obliterate them entirely. Feeling like semi-gods, they looked down over the red-orange scythe of lights created by traffic far below on the freeway. And to the west the expanse of Elliot Bay was intersected by ferries taking commuters home to the islands in the sound and on the peninsula.

Leigh sipped the wine she was offered, nibbled at delicious canapés and surveyed their fellow diners. An assortment of expensively suited businessmen, a sprinkling of wives. There were half a dozen uniformed types, clearly Ben's fellow pilots, and a bevy of extremely sophisticated young women. Secretaries? Flight attendants? One woman, in particular, caught her eye, a tall figure with vivid coloring and the sort of shape a man might dream about. At least twice she caught the girl watching her in a manner that was coolly assessing.

The wine helped to quell her feelings of panic and somehow the presence of other men in uniforms made Ben seem less extraordinary. It allowed her long-time sense of abandonment to resume more realistic proportions.

Ben helped, too. He looked after her like a cherished object d'art, introducing her with pride to his captain, Paddy O'Hare, to the chief test pilot, other engineers and TransOz personnel. They all accepted her with considerable courtesy and a fair bit of curiosity. However, only one co-pilot commented slyly on Ben's speed in acquiring an American girlfriend.

Shortly before the meal was announced, and during a gap in the general talk, Leigh asked, "Ben, who's that?"

He followed her gaze. "That's Tibor Szep. Our Chairman. He's also our major shareholder, but that's a by-the-by. Stinkingly rich. Has the reputation for being something of a maverick. That other guy with him is Jimmy Black, our Chief Engineer."

Tibor Szep was a remarkable figure, and not simply because of his size. He was a giant of a man, built like a linebacker, and not even the expensive tailoring of his suit quite masked the bull strength of those shoulders.

"He came to Australia just after the last war, without a penny to his name," Ben continued. "Now he owns major stock in TransOz, a world wide haulage business and has goodness knows how many irons in the fire."

"Is he a friend of yours?"

"Bloody hell, no!" Ben was amazed at the suggestion. "TransOz employs hundreds of pilots and I'm way down on the totem pole. He wouldn't know me from Adam. Why do you ask?"

"No reason," Leigh replied. "He's looked this way a couple of times and sort of smiled at me. I thought he must know you."

Dinner was announced at that moment.

She was sitting between Ben and his captain. Across the table sat the sophisticated woman with the vivid coloring and ravishing body. She was one of the senior TransOz stewardesses, Noeline Williams. She dominated most of the dinner table conversation in a voice which was overloud and a manner which excluded Leigh totally, while intimately involving the three men within her orbit.

Without bothering to draw breath Noeline expressed her views on America in general, and on Seattle and its miserable weather in particular. It had rained for all three days since her arrival. While they were still absorbing this barrage, she launched into her opinion of the present state and future prospects of TransOz.

None of this mattered. Leigh was enjoying her food sufficiently to desire no part in the conversation, but she was surprised that the three pilots were content to allow it. Surely such a monopoly of the table talk must be ill mannered, in whichever country you were. Even mildly expressed opinions at variance with hers were met with scarcely concealed scorn. Once Leigh caught Paddy O'Hare's eye while Noeline was holding forth on the interior configuration of the 747, clearly designed by a man, with absolutely no consideration for the conditions air hostesses have to tolerate. And to Leigh's amazement the captain winked at her.

It made her feel accepted, that wink. It suggested that, like her, Paddy could have consigned Noeline and her views cheerfully to the garbage heap.

After the meal came the ceremony. There was a speech by the chairman. Tibor Szep was presented with the keys of the first new plane. In exchange he presented Boeing with a picture by an Aboriginal artist. The keys, from this distance, could have been any set of car keys, and once again Leigh wondered just how one switched on those immense jet engines. Noeline, she noticed, took very little interest in the exchange. She made no attempt to mask her boredom, yawning twice without apology and inspecting minutely the perfection of her nail polish.

With the small ritual over everybody again merged. Ben and Leigh were engaged in idle conversation with Ben's captain when Leigh suddenly looked up. Tibor Szep was descending upon them, for all the world like the mountain which Mohammed sought. People parted to allow room for his royal progress across the thick carpet. He was a large man seen from afar; close to, his very bulk interfered with the passage of light.

He spoke in heavily accented English. "Aha, Benjamin. I see that you have not let the grass grow under your feet. And that is very good for international relations."

"Yessir! er, no, Sir!" Ben stuttered, amazed and a bit appalled that the great Tibor should have separated him out from the herd for attention.

"And what is the name of this beautiful young lady?"

In his confusion Ben stumbled over his own tongue. "Leigh. Leigh De St. Croix. No, no. I mean Leigh Pendleton."

It was hard to read what Tibor was thinking. His expression was totally enigmatic, even when presented with a young woman who answered to more than one name. He took her chin very gently in one vast hand and looked down at her. "Welcome to this little occasion, beautiful Leigh. We are pleased to have you here." His eyes switched from her to Ben, then back again. "And be very good to this young man, my dear. We need him."

He patted her gently on the shoulder and moved away.

"Well . . . !" drawled the captain, releasing his breath slowly as the huge figure retreated. "What on earth brought that on? And how the hell does he know your name?"

But Ben, still scarlet faced with embarrassment, could come up with no reasonable reply.

■　■　■

Fortunately for everybody's comfort, Noeline Williams appeared to be otherwise occupied during the remainder of the evening. So it was all the more annoying that Leigh should find her, some time later, in the beautifully appointed Ladies Room. When she realized that they were alone Leigh's first instinct was to withdraw immediately. She had seen nothing about the woman which prompted any desire to know her further. Unfortunately, Noeline glanced up from the hand basin with the opening of the door, saw Leigh's reflection in the glass, and she was trapped. The stewardess was still there when she emerged to wash her hands several minutes later.

"And what does it feel like, being the one in Seattle?" Noeline asked. It was the first time she had acknowledged Leigh's presence all evening.

"What?" Leigh pumped a small amount of liquid soap from the container.

"I said, 'What does it feel like being the one in Seattle?'"

"I'm afraid I don't follow you."

"Surely you've heard about pilots and their reputation?"

Leigh stopped washing and remained silent.

"Well, you know about sailors, don't you? A girl in every port? Pilots are the same, only more so. Everybody know that. Randy as alley cats, pilots are."

"Really." She knew now why she loathed Noeline Williams. She would not give her any room to continue this demeaning exchange.

But Noeline didn't require anyone's permission. Just as she'd ridden roughshod over all other attempts at conversation during the meal, now she refused to accept Leigh's dismissal of her.

"Really. We all know that, in the airline business. And Ben Beresford's the hottest of all. Ten, on our scale. He's a member of the Mile High Club. So, how does it feel to be his Seattle girl?"

Leigh's glance was so cold it would have stopped a lesser female, dead in her tracks. "Just fine, thank you," she said crisply. "A laugh a minute. Although I guess you must have been misinformed. Ben is a family friend. Perhaps you should check on your sources, before you leap to conclusions."

And she swept with all the dignity she could muster out into the lobby.

Ten

en was at a loss. He felt that he'd worked his soul
out to ensure Leigh enjoyed the evening. He'd
seen her visibly relax as the dinner progressed; he could have
sworn she was having a good time. Yet here she was, about
to leave the Columbus Club and looking for all the world as
though the cat had got her tongue.

Heading towards the floating bridge and the Eastside,
he realized that in scarcely two weeks he'd come to know
these roads quite well. However, he'd pretty much run
through his supply of conversational trivia on the outward
journey. By the time he reached the Kirkland waterfront,
and the small park where he'd parked previously, he, as well
as Leigh, had all but dried up.

The park was a far cry from the romantically moonlit

place of their previous date. Even the immediate point of land across the bay was obscured by drizzle which had settled in with the unrelenting determination well known to those who live in the great Northwest. But this was his last night in Seattle, and the weather, along with Leigh's oppressive silence, was just too bad. He had this overriding feeling that the time allotted him was running out. He switched off the engine.

"Listen, Leigh," he began, talking to the top of her head as she sat with eyes averted. "When you get home tonight I want you to take out your calendar for next year and circle the twentieth of February."

"What's so significant about that date?" It must be the next time he was coming into town. Maybe another delivery date. February seemed a lifetime away, the twentieth a remote and blank day in the future.

Ben, having released the confines of the seatbelt, took her chin and gently turned her to face him in the dim light. "It's a date of great significance. Precisely two thousand days from when I first met you. In San Francisco. You do remember that evening?"

"Sure. My engagement party. Paula threw it for us, when they still lived on Nob Hill. You came with David and Jane."

"Yes. I told you before how important it was to me."

"And I told you that trying to preserve a memory is ridiculous, because we all change. So, what else is significant?"

It was hard to see Ben's expression in the gloom.

His voice was very quiet. "Because I'm giving you plenty of time to get used to the idea. On the twentieth of February I'll be asking you to marry me."

Leigh wrenched her face from his fingers. "And is this

just another part of your little seduction game?" She was suddenly furious. "Exactly how many girls are privileged to receive proposals from Ben Beresford the Hot? Is it another of your carefully orchestrated plans? How cheap can you get. Do you count them on both hands, or as notches on your belt?"

Ben was staggered. "What are you talking about? What plans? What notches?"

"Scalps, then, or conquests! How do I know?"

In an attempt to quell the flow of scorn Ben took both of her hands firmly in his. He resisted her efforts to break free. "Leigh, what's this all about?"

Her outburst of rage was short lived. It was oozing away, leaving her shaky and vulnerable. "Don't even try to pretend I'm anything special to you. I know men like you. You see me the way you see all other women. Just as another conquest waiting to happen."

"If I did think of you like that you've proven me wrong many times over!" Ben exclaimed. "Talk to me, Leigh. Tell me what this is about."

By way of reply she burst into tears.

He hated the seats in this car before. Now he hated them a thousand-fold. Awkwardly he delved into his pocket for a handkerchief and handed it to her. Leigh mopped at her eyes. Fishing about for some reason why his heartfelt, carefully thought out preliminary proposal was being shoved back in his teeth with such scorn, he said tentatively, "You didn't imagine that I led a celibate life, did you? I never said that, did I?"

"Of course not." She gulped between her sobs. "But I just thought you were a normal guy. Not the airline stud, going to bed with everybody in sight."

"Who told you that?"

Leigh didn't reply directly. It was all becoming so hopelessly intertwined and entangled. All the conflicting images of the men in her life. And, throughout, there were her mother's words drumming away in her skull like the hideous throb of a headache. Finally she spoke. "Noeline Williams. Is she your girlfriend?"

"Noeline Williams?" Ben was suddenly alert. "Did she tell you that?"

"She didn't have to. I just knew, when I saw her."

Ben said awkwardly, "Leigh, I went out with her a few times. That's all."

"And went to bed with her?"

He winced. "Yes."

"And with other stewardesses, too? Not to mention all the girls in the other cities you fly into?"

"Of course not." Only partly true, he'd been pretty selective.

Leigh mumbled into the now sodden handkerchief. "I don't believe you."

Ben's bewilderment was fast consolidating into anger. It cleared his mind remarkably. Having recognized the insidious influence of Noeline Williams he prepared to mount a counter charge. "Leigh, listen to me. Just listen. I called you that first time because Jane suggested it, and I felt sorry for you, having lost Pete and all. I explained to you that I'd always remembered you, and why. I asked you out the next time because I liked you. And I thought the feeling was mutual." He paused. "Have I given you the slightest reason to suspect that my only motive for seeing you was lust?"

"Nancy says . . ."

"Forget what Nancy says! If I'd been after your body I'd have given up the pursuit some time ago."

Silence hung heavy, as laden as the air outside.

Ben was the first to speak. "All right. Can I tell you about Noeline?" He was greeted with silence, but pressed ahead. "She's one of the most senior stewardesses, which means she's been about forever and flies the premier routes. It's something of a joke about exactly how long it'll take for her to make a pass at a new pilot. I know that sounds grubby, but I'm trying to explain honestly. Noeline is a battle scarred old sheila, and she knows the ground rules. Or that's what I was told. When she gave me the 'come hither' about six months ago I thought I was merely another in the line. It just so happened that she fancied me, I suppose. Anyway, when it became apparent that she wasn't simply playing the musical beds game I finished with her. It ended more than two months ago, and I've not taken her out since. That's the truth, Leigh."

"And the other girls?"

"Sweetheart, of course there were other girls. I'm not a saint. But this is one thing I promise, when I ask you to marry me on the twentieth of February, it'll be the first time I've ever asked. Do you believe that?"

"I guess. If you say so."

"And you'll think about it?"

"Mmm."

"Just say that you like me. Say the words, 'I like you, Ben.' That'd be a start."

Very quietly. "I like you, Ben."

■ ■ ■

It was a most unsatisfactory end to an evening on which he'd embarked with such high hopes, but perhaps progress was made, after all. Maybe he'd set his sights too high, been unrealistic in his aspirations. Leigh was rather like a wounded animal, she needed infinitely gentle handling. Remembering her skunk of a husband he'd probably hit upon the nub of the matter. How could you emerge from a marriage such as Leigh's without being wounded?

Of course Nancy would be holed up in the apartment. They would have to say good-bye in that crummy little lobby which stank so badly of cat. Goodness knew when he'd manage to get back to Seattle again. He had no real way of knowing that she even accepted what he'd said. Curses to be heaped on the head of Noeline Williams as well as the head of Good Friend Nancy. Curses on the ghost of Pete Pendleton and Leigh's goddamn mother, come to that. Curses on anybody who hindered the path which he planned for them.

Standing in the shelter of the porch Ben drew her against him in a close hug, crushing the jasmine pinned on her shoulder. He rested his cheek against the short cap of shiny, brown hair and drank in the lingering smell of the bruised flowers.

"Ben."

"Yes?"

"My cheek. Your uniform's scratchy."

He grinned and released her slightly from his hug. "It wasn't such a bad evening, was it? Apart from Noeline?"

"I enjoyed the dinner. Really. And meeting your captain, and Mr. Szep."

"And you'll think about the twentieth of February? I'll call, but I'm awful on the phone. And I'll write, but I'm even worse with a pen. You're just going to have to trust me. Will you do that?"

Leigh did not reply, but Ben read at least conditional acceptance in her silence.

■ ■ ■

At about twelve-thirty the next day Leigh watched a silver plane rise from the general area of SeaTac Airport, make a wide arc over the city and turn south. It was too far away to see whether it had the distinctive gum-leaf motif of TransOz on the tail, but the time was about right, if they weren't delayed.

Eleven

*B*en had scarcely dumped his laundry in the linen basket when he phoned Jane. "Hello. How are my nieces? Are you treating them properly?"

"They appear to be thriving despite my regimen of starvation and torture. How was Seattle? Did you get in touch with Leigh?"

Amazing that in the last two-and-a-half weeks his life had turned about and taken a totally new direction, unknown to the family. "Yeah. I saw her. You didn't mention a son."

"Is that my cue to say, 'Oops! Sorry?' "

Ben laughed. "Of course not. Can I come up to see you? Soon?"

"Does 'you' mean me, or me-and-Dave, or me-and-

Dave-and-the-girls?"

"All of them, of course, but principally you."

"And which hat should I be wearing? Doctor's? Sister's? Agony aunt's? Or none of the aforementioned?"

"None and all," he replied. "Shall we say advisor's? Or counselor's?"

"Sounds serious."

■ ■ ■

Sydney, like so many modern cities, sprawls for miles across a vast, alluvial plain. That was why the journey from where Ben lived, overlooking the harbor on Cremorne Point, to where Jane and David had their house up in Springwood, took so long.

Once you were away from the suburban spread, and the township of Castle Hill, it became nearly pastoral. The road wound through Windsor and Richmond and finally climbed steeply up the escarpment which was a precursor to the Blue Mountains. Much of it was a pretty drive. The drawback was simply one of inaccessibility. It was too far away.

As he drove Ben thought again about how clever Dave was to have married Jane. He really admired him for his choice of wife. Jane was a truly remarkable woman, one of infinite depths and abilities She nurtured and sustained, she was wise and clever and wonderful. And Ben knew, to his everlasting shame, that never in a million years would he have been able to select her out of the crowd for those very qualities which he so appreciated. For physical attributes were far too important to Ben, and not even her nearest and dearest would claim that Jane was even moderately blessed in that direction. She was a large, lumpy woman, who had become larger and lumpier with each childbirth.

Her two abiding assets were her hair, which was red-gold and abundant, and her level, intelligent gray eyes.

David, who was after all a Beresford, and the oldest of the three to boot, could have chosen to be his life-mate any one of dozens of fellow medical students, not to mention hundreds of delightful and available nurses. Instead he saw fit to woo and win Plain Jane Bowen. And for his clear sightedness won the admiration and respect of his younger brother.

Jane called to him. "Come in. I've got the kettle on, and I've sent Dave out with the girls so we have the time to ourselves. I told him it was compulsory bonding time. What's up? Are you still eager to spill the beans?"

Ben, she knew, wasn't too good at confiding, even to as sympathetic a counselor as she was.

They went into the small, cluttered room which served as a study, and in which were housed with meticulous care many of David's research papers. It was the only room out of bounds for the girls. Jane plonked the tea tray down on the desk, herself on the large chair behind the desk. The chair groaned slightly but withstood the test.

Ben talked slowly, stumbling a bit as he tried to explain why he had sought her out. He sipped his tea between snatches of thought. "I went to see Leigh. She's living with the kid in this grotty apartment block, which should have been razed years ago as a health hazard. But that's not really a problem, or not long-term, because it sounds as if her in-laws might help out soon." He went on to explain the straitened circumstances which followed Pete's death.

Jane listened quietly, doodling, as was her way, on the pad of paper before her. "But you reckon all that's resolved, now?" She watched as Ben poured himself another cup of tea. The notion had flitted through her head that he might be about to hand round the hat on behalf of Leigh Pendleton.

"Yes."

"And how is she, in herself? Still grieving? It must be about six or seven months, now, since the accident. That's not very long, in terms of grief."

"Nearer nine months: not long after Christmas. I didn't get the feeling that she was still mourning him. She did talk quite a bit, about how he was as a father, rather than as a husband. From that I'd say she was well shot of the guy."

Jane was putting a very decorative hat on the rabbit which had materialized on the paper under her ball-point tip. "Just because you may not have thought much of him doesn't detract from Leigh's sense of loss."

"I realize that."

"So, did you see her again? Where do I come into this?"

"Jane . . . I'm in love with her."

The pen halted in the middle of a very ornate flower on Mrs. Rabbit's hat. "In love, little brother?"

"Yes."

"Not, as on the last half-dozen occasions, in lust?"

"No. In love. Honestly. I've sort of asked her to marry me."

The rabbit was being given a companion with inordinately large ears and gigantic buck-teeth. Anybody analyzing Jane's doodles would have field day. "And how does one sort of ask someone to marry one? On the contingency plan? Or by installment?"

Ben grinned. "In a way that's why I'm here to ask your advice. What I've done is give her warning that I'll propose, properly, next year. On the twentieth of February, actually."

"The twentieth of February. A milestone which leaps to the forefront of my mind for its obviously romantic connections. You've missed Valentine's day by a full six days there, Benjamin."

"The only significance is that it will be exactly two thousand days from that party on Nob Hill. The one where I first met her."

"Ah." Jane began to give the rabbit pair a large family of baby rabbits.

Ben had come to the tricky part, so he paused. It was awkward to explain because, despite a good deal of wrestling with it, he couldn't fully understand the circumstances which motivated Leigh. "It's my impression that the marriage was rotten, although she didn't absolutely spell it out." He stirred more sugar into his tea while he tried to pinpoint the important facts. "But she's let down her hair about all manner of other things. Did you know that her parents divorced when she was five? And that she's never had sight nor sound of her father from that day?"

"Tell me more."

"The mother sounds like a bitch of the first order, and, far worse, she's managed to persuade Leigh that all men are whoring lechers. Drummed it into her from the day Pa walked out, as far as I could gather. Leigh only half believes it, I think, because she's prepared to make jokes about it, until something turns up to knock her off balance. And then, there's this bloody friend. "

"Ben!"

"Sorry. But she really gets under my skin. Leigh's for ever quoting her. 'Nancy says this . . .' 'Nancy says that. . .' All of it violently anti-male clap-trap. Seriously, I could wring Nancy's neck."

The rabbit family had been discarded. Jane's pen was

now creating a fine display of leaves and flowers which might or might not be roses. "Let's backtrack a little," she said. "From all this exchange of confidences I gather Leigh's not averse to your courtship? And how can I put this delicately? Did you . . . ? Did she . . . ?"

Ben grinned. "The answer is no. I never even got near to trying."

"Very sensible, too. After all, who can tell where you've been?"

"Nowhere that caused the TransOz doctor to wag his finger or shake his head at me," Ben replied sanguinely. He sketched in the occasions when they'd gone out, the meal at the Space Needle, the picnic, the banquet at the Columbus Club. He even told her about Noeline. "There was one of the senior stewardesses. I had a bit of a thing going with her for a while, very casual, and all well and truly over weeks ago. She must have bearded Leigh in the cloakroom, because after that the evening went to hell in a handbasket. Noeline managed to suggest to Leigh that I spent my life fornicating with every sheila I could lay my paws on."

Jane did not look up from her pad. "Fancy that."

"Come off it!" Ben exploded. "Be fair." Then he noticed the twinkle in his sister-in-law's eye and subsided.

"Tell me about the little boy. Young Peter."

Ben made a face. "He's a clone of his father. Clingy little stinker, too. Not a patch on your girls."

Jane's tone was severe. "Millie and Janna did not lose their father less than a year ago. And even the loss of someone who's not exactly a perfect father can be very traumatic to a small child."

"I guess."

"And if you care for the mother, it goes without saying that you have to accept the child, too. And I mean 'accept.'

Whole heartedly. No ifs and buts. No maybes."

Ben, pounding a soft tattoo on the desktop with his fingertips, said again, "I guess."

"And you really love her?"

"Yes."

"The forever-and-ever love?"

"I reckon."

"Then what's to be done?"

"I don't know. How do I break through all that distrust, all those barriers? I don't know how to reach her. That's why I'm here, to ask your advice."

Jane doodled in silence for a few minutes. Then she sat back and pushed her pad across the desk towards Ben. "Sometimes my most intuitive rationalizing comes through my pen, you know. It's a fact. Do you see what I've drawn?"

Ben didn't want to insult her intuition or her drawing, but he could find very little connection between an enormous family of rabbits and Leigh's inherent distrust of the male gender.

"Bunnies?"

"Not the bunnies, dimwit. The hedge."

"Oh." That was a hedge, then.

"It came to me as you were talking. It's Sleeping Beauty, all over again. The modern version of course."

"Roses and thorns and things?" His voice sounded skeptical. Had dear, sensible Jane actually dropped off the twig?

"Don't be dumb, Ben. Think about it. Of course, Leigh isn't surrounded by a hedge of thorns, or roses; whichever version you fancy. But the mistrust she's built up. That's equally as impenetrable as any hedge. For the original evil fairy who cast the spell there's the mother, sowing the seeds, as it were. And then there's the man-hating chum fertilizing the thorn bushes like billy-o. Add a touch of growth hormone supplied by your discarded woman, and, voila! Do you see the analogy?"

"I suppose. But where does it leave me? Not kitted out in velvet, wearing pantyhose, I hope!"

"No, but you've probably got your work cut out for you, if you're serious about her. Are you?"

"More serious than anything else in my life."

Jane nodded. "Good. Then we have to prepare your sword. Get it polished and sharpened up. I must say, you'll have my support as you gird your loins about you."

"Ouch," Ben complained, "Girding my loins! That sounds painful."

She dismissed his protest. "Do whatever princes do in fairy stories. But I'll tell you this, little brother, I'll adore having Leigh Pendleton as a sister-in-law."

■ ■ ■

Later that evening, as she was brushing her hair before climbing into bed, Jane said, "Dave?" In a voluminous white nightie Jane looked like Britannia preparing to rule the waves.

"Darling?"

He was a wonderful husband. Jane knew he'd been simply bursting with curiosity to know exactly why Ben had driven for over two hours to talk to his wife. And there was no jealousy in him either, no snide references as to why Ben should select her as confidante ahead of his parents or brothers. Yet the whole time, since he and the girls had returned from their visit to the playground, and the evening assumed the normal course of all of Ben's visits, until this minute, he'd refrained from fishing for even one tiny clue.

"Young Benjamin."

"Mmm?"

"He's growing up."

David emerged from the bathroom and planted a passing kiss on the top of her red-gold hair. "It comes to us all, given time. What's your proof?"

"He's actually found someone he cares about more than himself."

"You don't say?" Ben's casual affairs, insofar as they impinged upon the family circle, were a matter of a fair bit of discussion. "And?"

"And he's got his work cut out for him. The girl is Leigh Pendleton. And believe me, he's fallen hard."

"Leigh Pendleton? That lovely girl? Wow!"

"More than 'wow'. I'm too tired to tell you more tonight, so you'll have to bite your fingernails overnight. But darling?"

"Yes?"

"I have a feeling this will be the making of your baby brother!"

Twelve

"How many roses?" Nancy asked. The vase of long-stemmed roses dominated the little dining table. Most were a clear pink, the gently curling outer petals tinged with cream.

"Twenty-two, actually." Leigh replied as casually as she could.

"And what's the significance of the two white ones?"

"I'm not sure exactly." And that was a lie.

"And these are from you-know-who who's out of your hair and separated from you by the Pacific Ocean?"

"Yes."

"And who means absolutely nothing to you?'

"I always said he was kind," Leigh hedged, finding the whole conversation embarrassing. She should have anticipated Nancy's dropping in and put the roses out of sight in her bedroom. But they were beautiful; they certainly did something for that miserable little room.

"Now you listen to your Aunt Nancy. Guys don't buy twenty-two roses out of feelings of kindness. That's not the motivating force, believe me."

"Nance, they're here. He isn't. Can we drop it? Let me get you some coffee."

It was hard for Nancy to drop any subject. In her capacity as President of Emotional Addicts Anonymous she tried the oblique approach. "I knew a guy once, a real hunk. Worked on the oil rigs out in the Gulf. Had pecs you could get lost in, and was a good listener, too. But he couldn't hold his booze. Two Jack Daniels down the road and he became Frankenstein's Monster. Belted the shit out of me, after a couple of little nips. What you might call a volatile fellow."

Leigh didn't really believe that the cute oil rigger existed outside Nancy's imagination. She could anticipate the answer to her question before she voiced it, but was prepared to go along with the story rather than face further interrogation about the significance of the twenty-two roses. "Why did you stay with him?"

Nancy's glance was patronizing in its scorn. She rolled her eyes heavenwards. "The bed, of course. That guy was dynamite in the sack."

This was well traveled territory. "I keep on telling you, Nance, I don't enjoy sex. Not at all. That's where we differ, you and I. You have this great appetite for it, which is what makes you vulnerable to men. I don't, so I'm not."

She missed Ben far more than she cared to admit. But the bit about sex was no fib, and was one reason she'd decided not to allow him any closer.

He'd phoned twice since his return to Australia, his voice bouncing off a satellite somewhere high above the Pacific and sounding in its clarity as if he were in the next door room. Their conversations weren't memorable, but she found herself looking forward to the sound of the bell quite against her better judgment.

There was one letter too, which confirmed his 'sweated labor' confession. But, literary masterpiece though it might not be, the message it conveyed was unmistakable. She had approximately one hundred and fifty days to come up with firmly rational, well thought out reasons as to why she was rejecting his proposal of marriage.

One hundred and forty-eight, as of today.

They sounded so reasonable when she rehearsed them in her head, those arguments in favor of staying single: God grant that she could parade them with equal logic when the time came. And, with luck, his schedule would be such that he'd be well away from Seattle for the foreseeable future. To suggest that he might never come back was taking 'hopefully' a bit too far. Anyway, with pilots who could tell? Perhaps not a girl in absolutely every city, but there were always stewardesses on hand. Given time, would he decide she wasn't worth all the effort and look for someone more accessible? That might save them both a lot of anguish, in the long run.

Nancy might have been privy to her thoughts. "I read a story once, about a pilot. In True Confessions. That guy was screwing every girl came his way. Ended up with AIDS. You gotta be careful of that, too, these days. Insist on a condom and ask to see his clean bill of health." Sex reappeared in Nancy's conversation with the regularity of a metronome.

Leigh kicked off her shoes and drew her legs under her on the sofa. "He still doesn't like Peter. I know you suggested rivalry, but I don't think that's at the bottom of it. Although I can't come up with any better reason. Even during that picnic at Deception Pass I felt caught in the middle."

Nancy pounced. "It's a rejection of you." She made her announcement as if declaring an earth shattering truth, and added emphasis to her words with a rather grand sweep of her arm. Some of her coffee slopped onto the table and Leigh rose to find a cloth. "That's what it is. He doesn't realize it, but the subconscious refusal to accept your son is really him rejecting you. You oughta consider that, my friend."

Too easy, again. But what other reasoning could lie behind the mutual dislike of Peter and Ben? And wasn't that the pivotal argument, in the long run? Could she ever consider any man who didn't include Peter?

"Perhaps." Agreeing reluctantly she changed the subject. "Let's walk the boys down to the lake while it's still nice out. I've got some stale bread they can feed to the ducks."

■ ■ ■

Every fairy tale needs a Good Fairy, the one who waves a wand and with a couple of swishes turns pumpkins into coaches and rags into ball gowns. Few tales have a Good Fairy built along the lines of a Russian weight lifter, even if that girth is encased in several thousand dollars' worth of Saville Row tailoring.

Ben was lunching in the TransOz staff dining room when Tibor Szep put in an appearance. Tibor's Head Office and home were in Melbourne. He deigned to visit Sydney only occasionally, and was to be seen in the dining room even more rarely, so this alone was a matter of some moment. His small, sharp eyes swept the crowd and came to rest on Ben. He progressed towards him like a monarch about to bestow a knighthood, or a sentence of death.

"Aha. Benjamin. And how are you?"

Caught totally unaware and also in mid-mouthful, it took a supreme effort on Ben's part to prevent all that followed from deteriorating into a Monty Pythonesque farce. He swallowed, gulped, stood in a hurry, and managed to blurt out, "Great, sir. Tremendous."

"Good. Good." Tibor nodded his head sagely, as if he had expected no other answer. "And the girlfriend? The beautiful American?"

"I think she's fine, sir. I spoke to her the other day, on the phone."

"Yes." He paused, still looking speculatively at Ben, until that latter felt the color fire up his neck. "It is hard, is it not, conducting a love affair when one's *kedves* is on other side of the globe?"

"Yes, sir."

"The same with me. Here was I, a penniless young man in Australia, and there was my Magda, waiting for me in far away Hungary. How I remember. A hard time."

"Yes, sir."

Tibor gave him another searching, thoughtful look. "Well, well. We shall have to do something about it, then; shall we not? Love must be given a little push. Is that not so?"

Luckily he was addressing his last remarks to the two other employees at the table, thus sparing Ben, who was at a total loss, the problem of a reply. He turned away and the group took their seats at another of the dining tables, some distance away.

Paddy O'Hare, with whom Ben was lunching, turned

an expectant face to his companion. He raised an inquiring eyebrow.

"I told you before, Paddy. Until that Columbus Club dinner I'd only seen him on the telly. Never in person. Honest."

"What about your mother? Perhaps she knows him." Then he laughed as Ben, his color racing, leapt to defend the virtue of his mother. "No, I cry pax! Don't answer. But it is mighty strange, the interest he's shown in you."

With this final remark Ben was in full agreement.

■ ■ ■

Be that as it may, with the new flight schedule Ben found that he was on the roster to fly the Pacific routes. TransOz had only one flight across the Pacific. Into San Francisco one week, Los Angeles the next.

Although they were prestigious routes, and Ben was being given a mighty big hike up the totem pole with this new scheduling, it wasn't unalloyed joy. He'd been flying with Paddy for over six months. They'd built up a considerable camaraderie, as well as an excellent working relationship. His new captain was an unknown quantity, so he would be starting again to create that important bond.

But there were thirty-hour stopovers in San Francisco and two-day delays in Los Angeles. That was worth all the rest. He began to pore over timetables, seeking the right interconnecting flights. Seattle, after all, was no more than a hop up the coast. Would it be fair to drop in on Leigh unannounced? How would she react? Perhaps he could suggest that he sleep over, promising to be ever so chaste, of course.

In the end he phoned her from San Francisco. "I'll be in Seattle by six, at your place by six-thirty. Can you arrange the baby-sitter so we can go out to eat? Somewhere local, as I won't have a car." That would be a good excuse to spent the night.

"Oh, Ben. Yes, of course."

Just hearing her voice, knowing she was only a few hundred miles to the north, made him feel warm inside.

■ ■ ■

When she'd returned the telephone to its cradle Leigh put her hands on her burning cheeks. Twenty pink roses, two white; and four hour's notice. Talk about being swept off one's feet. What about all those carefully rehearsed, ever so gentle put-downs? She'd fallen at the first hurdle. So much for good resolutions.

Thirteen

*F*our hours wasn't enough time to consolidate her arguments and prepare her defenses. That Leigh managed it spoke wonders for her determination. She anticipated Ben's arrival with the same mixture of dread and anxiety which generally preceded a visit to the dentist.

Nancy was out of town, so Leigh asked one of her fellow teachers at the Bay Center to watch Peter. Jill was glad to step into the baby-sitting mode, the only proviso being that his mother have Peter safely tucked into his bed before she left.

After she hung up the phone Leigh returned to sorting through Peter's clothing. He was growing so fast, sprouting up like a bamboo shoot. His clothes were outgrown far before they were outworn. She gathered together the items which would be handed on to Goodwill as she marshaled her thoughts.

Her decision had been reached. Tonight she was resolved to finish whatever there was between herself and Ben. The weeks apart from him had been beneficial in strengthening her intent, aided by an injection of spinal steel from Nancy.

The pile of garments was quite large; pants and T-shirts, several sweats. She found a brown paper bag to put them in.

She knew she was heading for disaster. The more she allowed Ben to become a part of her life, a part of her future, the harder and more bitter would be their ultimate break up. She'd reached this decision by acknowledging that there were certain women, probably her mother, and certainly herself, for whom any partnership was doomed at inception. It was something to do with their make-up, that they were incapable of inspiring in their partners sufficient commitment to a monogamous existence. And sharing your man with the world, as she'd discovered, was humiliating at best. That was it. The failing was obviously within herself.

All this she thought out with care, needing only to rehash her arguments as she stored the last folded T-shirt back on the shelf. She planned to explain to Ben this evening. It would be said very pleasantly, because he was such a sweet guy. And she could point out, by way of reinforcement, her abysmal failure as a sexual partner.

■ ■ ■

While Leigh was preparing and polishing her armor, Ben was approaching Kirkland with emotions far less complicated, but plans equally well prepared. He'd even remembered Jane's advice sufficiently to pick up a small koala bear for Peter, one of those little toys which clasps your finger between its two front paws.

Being in love was a fantastic state, he'd discovered. It heightened all his senses, in the way he imagined LSD might do, if you were dumb enough to risk the flip side of that particular coin. He felt that he'd never before been so appreciative of beauty, so receptive to music, so awake. If only he could share half his enhanced sensory awareness with Leigh, explain to her how vital she was to his very being.

'Don't rush things,' Jane had warned. 'It's all very well to say that the prince barged headlong in, chopping away like billy-o. If you do so you'll find that your sleeping beauty has fled before you get there. Patience.'

All very well for Jane to preach. He had only limited time, and there was a bloody great puddle of water separating them.

Peter, clad in night attire, accompanied Leigh as she opened the door. "Hi there, Kiddo," Ben said. "I've brought you something from Australia."

Peter said nothing, just twined himself round his mother's legs and peered darkly at Ben.

"Say thank you, Punkin," Leigh urged. She wished that her son would outgrow this clinging stage.

Peter spoke in a muffled voice. "What is it?"

"It's a koala bear." Ben fished about in his pocket and located the little toy. "That's an animal we have in Australia, and see? The arms work like this."

Peter accepted the toy and inspected it in silence for a moment. Then he looked up. "Why are you dressed like that?"

"Punkin! That's not polite, commenting on someone's clothes."

Ben replied reasonably to a question he considered perfectly sensible. He tried to make his voice sound friendly, although even to his own ears it still came across as rather tight. "This is my uniform. I have to wear it when I'm flying, so that the passengers can identify me. Perhaps one day you can come to the airport and see the plane I fly."

The child accepted this without further need to investigate and left his mother's side to return to his cars and roads. The small koala lay abandoned on the table.

Ben was free to accord Leigh his full attention. He thought he'd remembered every detail of her appearance: now he realized that memory is a fickle tool. She was far more beautiful when standing before him in the flesh. Love for her welled inside him like sweet water gushing from a spring. He wanted so badly to take her in his arms and express his adoration, but Jane had counseled patience. And there was something in her eyes, some expression he couldn't quite fathom.

"Nancy's down in Portland. Her Mom's sick," Leigh said. "I've asked a friend from work to stay with Peter, and she'll be here soon. Do you think you could read him a bedtime story while I finish in the kitchen?"

Peter and Ben eyed each other. "Of course." Even to his own ears Ben's voice sounded falsely hearty. "What shall we read, Kiddo?"

"I want my Mommy to read to me," Peter muttered sullenly.

"Punkin."

Ben decided that no kid was going to be allowed to ruin his precious evening. He ignored Peter's protest. "What shall we choose? 'Thomas the Tank Engine?' You know, my Mum used to read that to me and my brothers when I was your age. What do you say?"

Peter didn't fight. He allowed himself to be tucked into bed and Ben perched a little awkwardly on the edge. He finished chronicling the adventures of Thomas at about the same time that Leigh appeared to turn off the light.

They ate at a Thai restaurant because it was an easy walk down the road. Ben was aware that he'd been manipulated by fate. In suggesting that they eat at a restaurant he'd thought to get Leigh well clear of Nancy's accidental dropping-in. With Nancy safely in Portland they could as easily have ordered pizza at home, cozily domestic. However, he accepted the turn of events in good part, and appreciated the food.

He was buoyed up by the sight of twenty-two roses well past their prime date, still occupying pride of place on the table.

■　■　■

Leigh picked at her food, not because it wasn't delicious, but because she was fighting an internal battle with herself which took most of her concentration.

Having reached certain painful but correct decisions, it was very upsetting to discover afresh how attractive Ben was. How attracted she was to him. Those blue eyes which seemed to smile, that particular masculine aura. Even the uniform was on his side. It wasn't half as difficult, this time around.

She launched into her rational, intelligent, thoughtfully reasoned explanation as to why this was The End as they walked back up the hill. The evening was two dimensional in its stillness. Early fall, a high cloud obscuring the moon, no wind, not even a whisper of breeze. As if the earth's cycle was on hold.

Having made a good start, she finally reached the part when she could explain how it was a fault in her, not in him. It was a bit galling when Ben interrupted.

"What the hell are you talking about? You're incapable of keeping a guy's love? This is utter tosh!"

"No it's not. It's the truth. There are some people like that. My mother . . . "

"I know about your parents; and they're a separate issue. What makes you think like that? Why are you so certain that the fault is yours?"

"Pete . . ."

"Pete."

"Yes. Will you let me explain?"

Ben decided that this was not the time to return to the apartment. There'd be the business of getting rid of the baby-sitting chum. He took her hand and turned them about, heading slowly towards the waterfront.

"All the explanations you like," he said. "Take as long as you need. You're warm enough?" Leigh nodded. "But I give you fair warning, I'm going to mount a counter-attack."

They leaned against the railings which skirted the lakefront. The water was still and muted with the slight sheen of long neglected gunmetal. The far shore was simply a blur of darker gray on the horizon.

Ben held her hand warmly in his. "Fire away."

Even with this encouragement Leigh found it hard to start. "I suppose it has to go back to my Mom. She's probably responsible for making me distrust men. And she thought it was the right thing, ensuring I wasn't going out into the world a starry-eyed innocent. But the fact is, I really was just that. An honest-to-Betsy starry-eyed dope. Pete came into the picture in my last year at Berkeley. I thought he was absolutely wonderful. I rationalized that Mom's views were twisted because of my dad, and that, anyway, we'd be different. You know how it is, you think the other person's experience never applies to you.

"Pete had the reputation for being a lady's man; but he promised that his womanizing days were over. Of course, I believed him. I wanted to believe him, so I simply shut my eyes to his flirting and his secrets. He was a great one for secrets. He explained quite reasonably that for a marriage to work we each needed to have our own space. He meant, of course, his own space. Not mine. My space was still to be accountable to him, because he could be ferociously jealous."

She paused in her narrative to brush her eyes. Ben realized that tears had gathered. He wanted very badly to gather her into his arms, but she was so terribly fragile.

"Does it hurt to tell me?" he asked gently.

Leigh took the handkerchief that he offered and wiped her eyes. "It hurts to remember how dumb I was. Less now, I guess, than before. I know it's a cliché, but time really does help, in the end. And you need to know, so that you'll understand my decision.

"In retrospect I guess he never gave up having girl-friends, but at the time I was too naíve to realize. I was busy playing 'House Beautiful', and later on Mommies and Daddies, while he was enjoying himself with every female around. It was so humiliating. Everybody else was fully aware of what was going on. Discretion was not in Pete's vocabulary.

"Finally I came to understand that, in a way, the fault was mine. I wasn't sufficiently brilliant and compelling to keep his interest. I couldn't satisfy him in bed. And somehow his playing around was a sort of wish fulfillment on my part. Does that make sense?"

Ben's first instinct was to say savagely, 'Yeah, as much sense as banging your head against a wall to cure a headache.' But he was far too aware that Leigh, in telling him all this, was exposing her tender underside, and needed all the reassurance he could find. "You take on too much guilt. There's only one thing to blame yourself for; you chose to fall for a jerk. After that everything was on automatic pilot."

Leigh blew her nose and smiled tremulously. "Maybe. The result is the same. And one of the most humiliating times came after the accident, when we were trying to sort out all the debts. I kept on coming across bills for this diamond bracelet, that lease on a Malibu apartment. All for other girls. And I had to explain to my father-in-law that none of these items was an asset I could liquidate. He looked at me, in that way he has, all fierce eyes and bushy eyebrows, as if it was entirely my fault. I was an utter failure as a wife. And I knew he was right. I was."

"Can I say 'utter tosh' now?"

"If you must."

■ ■ ■

Along the waterfront there was a cart still open, selling espresso coffee. Ben ought them each a cup. They returned to the railing to drink them. The coffee was dark and deliciously bitter.

"Is it my turn now?"

Leigh repeated, "If you must," but her tone implied, ' you're wasting your time.'

Ben decided that nothing would be gained in confessing to Leigh the tale of the engagement party. In this context it might not sound particularly amusing. He chose his words carefully, aware of how important this was. "Because you happened to fall for the wrong bloke last time is no reason to take a vow of eternal solitude. Not all fellows are non-stop fornicators."

"Tell me about it."

Aware of his track record he said soberly, "There's such a thing as trust."

"Tell me about that, too."

"I'd rather show you. But for it to work you have to take a leap of faith and give me the opportunity."

Leigh warmed her hands round the cardboard cup. "I can't do that. I can't afford to. I told you before, ages ago. I'm too scared. That's why I'm not going to see you again. We're better off, Peter and I, on our own."

"And I get consigned to the scrap heap? Thanks a bundle." His voice reflected his frustration.

"You'll find another girl before I fall asleep tonight. Someone far more suitable, one who's not damaged goods."

"I don't want another girl. I want Leigh of the Lovely Smile."

"She's dead. And buried."

He thought of those twenty-two withered roses, still sitting on the table. Leigh was a punctilious housekeeper. He decided to try another tack. "Can we reach a compromise?"

"Probably not."

"In the interests of fair play, what's cricket and all, you must agree I deserve a chance to prove myself. I know you only half believed what Noeline said, but there was a fair residue of suspicion just longing to burst forth, wasn't there? Can you accept that those other girls were only dry runs, while I waited for you to reappear in my life? And I need to prove that you can trust me. Is that fair?"

Leigh concentrated her gaze on the glassy surface of the

water. "Maybe. What are you proposing? Another dry run, this time with me?"

He let that remark ride. "You've got that date, the twentieth of February, on your calendar?" She kept her eyes averted. "Let me show you that I'm serious. You'll still receive my proposal, on that day. And if you say 'no', that will be the end. No more of me in your life. I'll probably enter a Buddhist monastery in Nepal, and spend the rest of my life there, but you'll be in the clear. Is that reasonable?"

A great rush of something akin to rage rose inside Leigh. She wanted to scream, 'You haven't heard a word I've said. Can't you accept that I'm frightened of falling for you, that I'm terrified of my own feelings?' How could she survive until the twentieth of February?

The silence seemed to last a lifetime. Leigh drained the last of her coffee. Then she sighed. "I guess. But there's something else you'd better know. I'm useless in bed. Frigid, I think."

"Another truth imparted by Pete?" The silence stretched. "I'll risk that too. But Leigh . . . ?"

"Yes?"

"The time until then is mine? I promise I'll not rush into your bed until you're ready. Cross-my-heart-and-hope-to-die."

Nancy would think she'd lost her marbles. Nancy, President of Emotional Addicts Anonymous would never forgive her. "Okay."

"And do I have to debunk to a hotel? Or can I sleep over tonight?"

"Only on the couch. And it's probably hideously uncomfortable."

Ben smiled. "I'll risk that, too."

Fourteen

he couch was hideously uncomfortable, just as
Leigh predicted.

Ben woke in the morning feeling that his back
belonged to another person and was his only because a series
of giant staples held it in place. Unfolding from the couch
took several minutes of painful maneuver; even a hot shower
mitigated the ache only in part.

There were some advantages inherent in not being
designated First Favorite, however. Were he shacking down
in Jane's and David's living room, his morning slumber
would have been rudely shattered by two small bodies
hurtling onto the bed at some ungodly hour and determined
to extract every ounce of pleasure from his visit.

In sharp contrast, Peter, still resentful and suspicious,

stood in the doorway clutching his blankie, and stared darkly at the intruder.

■ ■ ■

Ben set down his overnight bag by the door. "Leigh, next week. I'm on the L.A. flight, which gives me a forty hour lay-over. If the flight times don't change I'll be here by early evening, and we'll have all of Wednesday free. You don't work on Wednesdays, do you?"

"No."

"Then perhaps we can do something, if the weather's kind? I dunno what's available. What would you suggest?"

"The zoo, perhaps? It's not picnic weather."

Ben turned to Peter. "You'd like that, Kiddo? A visit to the zoo?"

Peter didn't reply, but turned questioning eyes to his mother. She answered for him. "You'd love it, Punkin, wouldn't you? Seeing the animals and petting them?"

They were waiting for Ben's taxi. The sound of a horn announced its arrival.

He was just about to depart when Leigh said, quite casually, as if it were a matter of very little importance, "By the way, we won't be here next week. We're moving. I meant to tell you."

"Moving! Where?"

"Not far from here. About half-a-mile along the waterfront."

"What brought that on so suddenly?"

In her single-minded determination to say good-bye to Ben for good, the fact that he might turn up next week to an empty apartment had almost escaped her.

"My in-laws, the Pendletons. They've agreed to pay me

child support. So I'm becoming their welfare recipient instead of the Government's." As an appendage she added a bit lamely, "I did mean to tell you."

Downstairs the horn beeped insistently.

"And the rest!" Ben exploded. "You meant to disappear without letting me know where to find you, that's what you meant. Well, it won't work. If you imagined for a minute I'd just let you drop out of sight without turning over every stone to find you you've got another think coming. From now on that's not in the rules. Understood?"

"Understood." Her contrition was absolutely genuine. She could see how her omission looked through his eyes. "I'm sorry, Ben. Really."

Another angry hoot. Ben glanced at his watch and swore under his breath. "I'll phone you from Sydney. I hope the move goes well. Bye, Kiddo. Bye, you impossible woman."

Some of the hurt he felt was in his kiss. It was hard and almost accusatory, more of a punishment than a caress.

■ ■ ■

There was something else she'd forgotten to mention in the face of all which had been said. And it was still pivotal. Ben's dislike of her son.

She found herself lying in bed each night, watching the pattern on the ceiling made by the lights of passing cars. Her thoughts would return to this same point with the regularity of toothache. It was like a throb that wouldn't leave her. She realized now that she should have raised the issue, once it was obvious that he was not prepared to accept her good-bye. In the absence of any other reason she'd been forced to conclude that Nancy was probably right. Ben's resentment was founded on jealousy. And if he rejected her son, didn't he, in a way, reject her, too? Certainly refuse to accept her in the role of mother.

It wasn't as if Peter were a difficult child, she rationalized. He was a bit clingy, at present, but common sense told her that many three-year-olds were inclined to cling. Peter would get over this stage, indeed he was already gaining in confidence. She was pretty sure Ben liked other children, because he'd actually shown her snapshots of himself with his nieces, where he was giving them piggyback rides, or they were burying him in the sand. That was not the behavior of a guy who considered children to be mere nuisances.

Leigh pulled the sheet under her chin and resolutely closed her eyes, willing sleep to come. But it was an issue that wouldn't lie down. It must be faced, because it was like a thorn turning septic in the flesh. A small hurt, perhaps, but potentially lethal.

■ ■ ■

The plans for the following week's visit were discussed and agreed over the phone. But, like many well laid plans, this particular scheme got off to a very rocky start. The airline business, perhaps more than any other, is vulnerable to the domino effect. On this occasion one unscheduled mishap caused ripples which widened at each following stage. A plane broke down in Singapore, another was sent to replace it. Delay incurred further delay until Ben's flight did not touch down in Los Angeles until just short of ten P.M.

It was a close call getting through immigration and onto the last connecting flight to Seattle. A very close call indeed.

The taxi drew up outside Leigh's new apartment complex some time after midnight. He couldn't see much in the dark, but the scant view he had, and the general approach to the block, told of a considerable improvement in the level of comfort. He had phoned to inform Leigh of the delayed flight, hoping she would wait up for his arrival.

In the intervening week Ben's anger had cooled somewhat, doused by an onrush of love. He refused to accept that Leigh might ever have intended to drop from view. It was more an oversight, understandable when he considered all the ground they'd covered the previous evening.

The new apartment was on the first floor. Leigh pressed the security lock and opened the door to him. She was wearing her usual sleep attire, which to Ben was no more than an exceptionally large T-shirt. It seemed only just to cover the necessary parts. Her face was free of all make-up. Her shortcut hair was ruffled and she looked a bit owlish, as if she'd been napping. Her legs were bare and smooth and slim. The tension of the moment sizzled between them like bacon on a skillet.

Ben was a normal, healthy young man with a normal supply of hormones. He was also deeply in love. For the last few weeks he'd kept his sexual urges strictly under the hatches, prompted by his determination to play his part as the prince strictly according to the rules. At that moment the rules were within a hair's breadth of being tossed out of the window.

This, in his fantasy world, was how the future would be. He would come home from a flight, the door would be opened by his wife, by Leigh. She would be waiting for him wearing just that T-shirt, welcoming him, unable to sleep with longing for him. They would kiss deeply, passionately, then go into the bedroom. The door would shut behind them. Heaven would follow.

"Leigh." His voice sounded hoarse, filled with gravel. "Honey, you look marvelous."

He didn't dare hug her, if he did there was no guarantee that the fantasy wouldn't get the better of his judgment. Instead he took her by the shoulders, very gently, and kissed her with great tenderness. "Have you missed me? Say you've missed me."

"I missed you, Ben."

Count to ten, Benjamin! Get a grip on yourself, dammit! One . . . two . . . three . . . Thoughts of ravishment were ebbing. "Now try again, with a bit more enthusiasm."

She smiled. "I missed you, Ben. Really. I could have done with some manpower to help with the move."

He steadied himself . . . eight . . . nine . . . ten. The dangerous moment was over, the prince was again in control. "Yeah, well we do have our uses." His voice was rueful. "Even if it's only lugging furniture down stairs."

■ ■ ■

After its ghastly predecessor the apartment was a little slice of luxury. The space was more than double, there were two bathrooms, a deck, a view over the lake, albeit some way in the distance. Leigh had retrieved some of her furniture, so there was actually a bed for Ben, in the guest room. After that couch it was bliss.

Even Peter seemed more accepting. He allowed Ben to tie his sneakers, at Leigh's request.

It was a perfect autumn day to visit the zoo. The rumblings of portending trouble came shortly after lunch as they made their way towards the petting corner. Peter was anxious to try the hands-on approach which his mother had promised. He released his hold on her fingers and skipped ahead eagerly.

"Watch it, Kiddo!" Ben called after the little fellow's fast disappearing back.

"His name is Peter," Leigh said tautly.

Ben recognized that something in her tone and glanced down at her. "Yes," he agreed, noncommittally.

"Then why don't you call him that?"

Ben prevaricated again. "You don't like me to call him Kiddo?"

"It's nothing to do with that. You simply avoid using his name, or having anything to do with him, if you can."

"I read to him. I put on his sneakers."

"Only because I asked you to."

All of which was true, but how could you attempt to explain the complexities of the issue when surrounded by happy families in the middle of the zoo? Ben glanced over at Peter who was busily engaged in making the acquaintance of an inquisitive young kid. The petting corner attendant was carefully explaining to him the niceties of how one approached animals.

He propped himself against the retaining fence. "Okay. I'll call him Peter, if you'd rather." It would take a mighty effort, but it would be worth it to please Leigh.

"That's evading the issue. And it's not just his name. I've seen those snapshots of you with Jane's girls, on your knee, having piggy-back rides. You never go anywhere near Peter unless I ask you to do something for him."

Ben said a little awkwardly, "Leigh, could we talk about this another time? Let's not spoil today."

But Leigh had the bit firmly clenched between her teeth. "Today is already spoiled," she replied tightly, thinking of all Nancy's sage words. "Because although you're full of talk about marriage proposals and the like, the truth is that when you reject my son you're rejecting me."

"That's balderdash, and you know it!"

"No it's not. Nancy says it's because you're jealous, and I think she's right."

He hated the thought that she discussed him with anyone, least of all with Nancy, the wicked witch of the west. "The hell with what Nancy says. Don't quote that baggage at me. And anyway, while we're on the subject, what about your rejection of me? Isn't this a two-way street?"

It was Leigh's turn to look directly at him. "You know that's not true. It's any relationship which scares me. I haven't rejected you. Not you, as a person."

"Oh no?"

Ben glanced around. Like most men he hated rows of any kind. The worst sort were those conducted in public. But this particular row at this time was being thrust upon him. Peter had abandoned the kids and progressed to the guinea-pig enclosure. He was fully absorbed, for the moment. There were, mercifully, no other flapping ears within range.

Even so, fearful of creating any sort of spectacle, Ben kept his voice low. "What about this? Instead of a normal wooing I'm doing my best-ever imitation of a crab, approaching a completely respectable, above the board marriage proposal sideways, as if what I'm offering you is something a bit icky and in poor taste." He ticked off the items on his fingers. "Next, you say you like me, but I'm rationed to the occasional kiss as a reward for good behavior, not a hint of anything more because you'd prefer to believe a trouble-maker like Noeline rather than trust me. Then, having established the ground rules with all the advantages on your side, you were perfectly happy to skip out of sight without as much as a hint that you'd be moving house . . ."

"But . . ."

"No buts. All this I could understand a bit better if you were still being loyal to the memory of a husband you loved."

"Ben . . ."

Again he ignored her interruption. "No. Your excuse is that all men are slugs who go whoring about. And why? Because you choose to listen to the Nancys and the Noelines; because they say what you want to hear, exactly as your mother used to. All of which you, of course, are hell bent on believing. So you lump the entire male population into the category of unreliable lechers, and hide behind that as an excuse. And then you have the nerve to accuse me of being jealous of your son!"

It was a remarkably long speech for Ben, and the strength of feeling he expressed left both of them bereft of words for a few minutes.

Then Leigh, not looking at him, said, stiffly and uncomfortably, "That's not an excuse, as I tried to explain to you. It's a reason."

"It's a bloody stupid reason."

"And I'm sorry about not mentioning our move. I would have let you know. Honest."

"Oh yeah?"

Peter ended the argument. He ran back to them, bubbly and excited. "Mommy, I petted the guinea-pigs! And the goat."

"That's great. Was it fun?"

"Yes. The guinea-pigs are all soft and furry. Their noses go wiggle-wiggle. And the goat tried to nibble my fingers. Can we get ice-cream?"

For Peter's benefit they finished the outing. They bought ice-creams, watched the waterfowl, marveled at the height of the giraffes. But the day was spoiled.

There was so much still needing to be said, but Ben had to get to SeaTac for his connecting flight. Somehow to half-start a topic and leave it unresolved was worse than not broaching the subject at all.

He changed into his uniform in the apartment while Leigh found useless things to do in the kitchen. "Next week . . ."

"Oh Ben, I'm sorry. We won't be here next week. I'm taking Peter to see his grandparents." Another sin of omission. How could she have been so careless? He'd never believe it was accidental, that she'd overlooked it in all the bustle of their move.

"Well, that's great. Thanks for telling me before I flew up from Frisco." His voice was savage. "What is this, Leigh? Some sort of obstacle course I'm supposed to weather? Some game with a new set of goal posts at each turn?"

"I said I'm sorry. I just didn't think . . ."

"Yeah. You can say that again. You just didn't think."

He ruffled Peter's hair lightly in farewell, kissed Leigh perfunctorily on the cheek. She accepted his caress impassively, longing to throw her arms round his neck, unable to do so.

"Good-bye, you crazy, mixed up woman," Ben said in farewell. "Just tell me this: how much more head banging am I expected to do before I'm allowed even a tiny chunk of your life?"

As he drove away he wondered bitterly if he'd been cast for the wrong role. Maybe he should have auditioned for the part of court jester. Perhaps he just wasn't cut out to be the prince, after all.

Fifteen

They did not see each other again for nearly a month. For differing reasons it was a wretched time for both.

Ben was flying the Western Pacific route, to Hong Kong and Singapore, which gave him no chance of a stopover in Seattle. And he found himself at odds with his new Captain over a matter of procedure, which added to his feelings of ill use.

Leigh was miserable. She'd concluded that perhaps Nancy wasn't always the most reliable consultant. Added to that, she was having a tough time sorting out the conflict caused by her very considerable attraction to Ben, and her equally strong feelings of mistrust in any binding relationship. Ben might be correct in saying it was a stupid reason, but he had never been married to Pete.

This was the sort of time when she longed for her mother. Certainly not the mother she had, who whiled away the hours amongst the idle rich of Newport Beach with revolting little Pookie and her smarmy gigolo in attendance. But the mother who should have been hers in a perfect world, the one who offered sensible, down-to-earth advice and provided more than Diaper Service when you gave her a grandson.

As a friend and confidant Nancy was reliable in many ways, but experience had left her so hostile that perhaps her views about relationships were a little suspect.

Of course, Ben called and they talked on the phone, which was better than nothing. But Ben, more inarticulate than usual because of the hurt he was feeling, could not bridge the gap and find the necessary words to patch things up.

Finally it was Leigh who set the ball rolling. "Ben, about that day at the zoo. I'm sorry our day was ruined."

"That's okay; I'm sorry too. I know you've been through rough waters. I shouldn't attempt to pressure you. Next time I'll try harder with Peter, I promise."

Leigh thought of her small son. He seemed so uncomplicated, easy to like, easy to love. "Ben, what is the problem? What is it about him that you don't like? It isn't jealousy, is it?"

Again Ben searched for the right words. He'd thought about this particular issue at some length, because he recognized its importance. However, expressing his conclusions wasn't so easy. "Perhaps it is, in a way. I mean, I'm not jealous that you have a son. And I love kids. It's the way he looks. His appearance. If he'd taken after you I'd have no problem at all. As it is, every time I lay eyes on him I see

Pete staring right back at me. And you're spot on, I'm bloody jealous of Pete. Dead and all." There, it was out.

"You're jealous of a dead man?"

"I'm jealous and I'm mad. Mad because he took that fabulous girl with the thousand-carat smile and hurt her and cheated on her and squeezed the joy out of her. Mad because I knew he was wrong for you, way back at the beginning, and I did nothing about it. And I remember all of that whenever I look at Peter. Or even say his name." He paused, then added savagely, "Why the hell didn't you call him Bob, or Jim?"

He could almost hear Leigh smile along the line. "Oh, Ben! Poor little boy. Is this what they mean when they say that the sins of the father are visited unto the third and fourth generation?"

Ben, relieved at least in part of his burden, could smile ruefully, too. "I dunno. Perhaps. Does all that I've said sound like tripe to you?"

"Yes. No. It does explain things. Why didn't you tell me sooner?"

"You know me. When it's important I'm hopeless at putting what I feel into words. A real idiot. It always sounds so stupid in my ears."

Leigh was pondering his confession. "It sounded just fine to me."

He changed tack. "Leigh, honey, you can't imagine how much I miss you."

She almost said, 'And I miss you too,' but he might misinterpret that. "Ben, thank you for telling me."

After she'd returned the phone to the cradle she went into the small bedroom which was Peter's, knelt down by the bed and contemplated her sleeping son.

When she considered him in that way, of course, he did

resemble his father, both in coloring and features. The same dark hair and eyes, the same cleft in the chin. But he had been her son from birth, and she saw him simply as a baby and a little boy, an evolving being. Not as the bearer of possibly unattractive genes. And, although he was still young, she could recognize very little of Pete in his personality.

Pete was always brimful of confidence and totally opinionated, perhaps because during his childhood each utterance had been considered as precious as a sacred pearl. Pete always ran roughshod over everybody and everything which stood in his path. That was his way.

His son was far less confident. He was more like her. And he was a sensitive child, recognized when she was feeling worried or down. On those occasions he would wrap his arms round her neck to offer comfort.

She stroked the silky hair back from his smooth brow and tucked his hands under the comforter. Two people who shared the same gender. All right, two men. Both were at present interwoven strands of her life. One she was totally responsible for, to whom she was irrevocably tied for at least the next fifteen-odd years. The other, with a remarkable magnetism, who was weaving his way into the fabric of her happiness. She wasn't prepared to accept that both might share her future, because a major factor in her scheme for self-preservation was the determination that never again would she lay herself open to such hurt. But even in the short term it was important to her that they like each other.

Well, at least she understood now exactly why Ben retreated each time from contact with her son, her 'pumpkin eater.' Understanding brought acceptance, and gave her an opportunity to deal with it.

■ ■ ■

When, finally, his flight schedule changed and Ben was able to squeeze in an overnight in Seattle, the occasion could not have been more calculated to kill romance.

Peter had come down with some nameless bug which made him feverish. Two days later he was still fretful and irritable. Three days of nursing and sleepless nights didn't do a great deal for Leigh, either, so Ben walked into an apartment in which the atmosphere was scarcely serene. He'd brought her roses. When she opened the door he took her in his arms and kissed her before she could find words of protest.

"How's the invalid?"

"Cranky."

"Must be on the mend, then. I've brought you both something from Hong Kong." He indicated the wrapped gifts in the bag he'd sensibly deposited by the door in order to have his arms free.

"Oh, Ben, you shouldn't. But, before we open them do you think you could sit with Peter for half-an-hour without killing him?"

"I might just manage that. What for?"

Leigh sighed. "Nancy's back visiting her folks in Portland. I've not left the apartment in four days. We're practically out of everything. I can't even offer you a beer"

"That seems the most sensible of all reasons. Curfew starts at nine and I can't drink after that, so get a move on."

"You don't mind?"

Ben squinted down at her. She was always amazed at the blueness of his eyes. "What do you want? An oath on the Bible that I'll not ritually slaughter the heir to the Pendleton Millions?"

She smiled, a small, tight gesture. "Actually, he's napping at present, and may sleep until I'm back. There's lemonade in the refrigerator, if he's thirsty."

Leaving Ben alone with a hard to please Peter wasn't her first choice, but she had little alternative. Like the cupboard of Old Mother Hubbard, hers was bare.

Ben prowled. He peered in the refrigerator, turned on the television to be confronted by an offering of innumerable soaps and nothing else, switched it off and idly skipped through a three days old paper.

He could hear stirrings from the bedroom and wondered if Peter would make a scene when he realized that his mother was not present. He'd put a considerable number of flying hours into confronting his feelings about the child. It was easier, now that it was out in the open, not gathering poison like an abscess inside him. And he was resolved to try to like the kid. He needed to forget about the loathed person who had sired him, to accept that as an unalterable fact and progress from there.

Peter was sitting up in bed, his hair tousled, his face crumpled from sleep. He looked flushed.

"Hello, Peter. How's things?"

The child stared darkly at Ben with hostile eyes. "Where's my Mommy? I want my Mommy."

That was part of the problem, too. Peter appeared to resent Ben almost as much as Ben resented him. Ben was used to Janna and Millie and Su leaping into his arms with every indication of delight, but he and Peter circled each other warily like two hunters stalking the prey. The only thing they had in common was Leigh. She was the pivot, central to their differing needs.

Ben, having covered this very ground many times and concluded that his own behavior was far more childish and unreasonable than that of any three year old, sat on the edge of the bed. "Your Mummy's gone shopping, Peter. She asked me to stay with you. She'll be back soon. Shall we get you dressed?"

The child held up his arms to let Ben slip a sweatshirt over his head. He said in conversational tones, "Why'd you call me Peter?" and then, not waiting for an answer, "I've been sick, but I'm better now."

"So your Mummy told me." Ben remembered the post-nap drill for the little girls. "Now, how about a trip to the bathroom? Do you need help?"

Peter replied with dignity, "I can go by myself. I'm three!" Afterwards he let Ben help him on with his pants.

■　■　■

Leigh, returning nearly an hour later, almost held her breath while she listened. At least neither was screaming.

Ben let her in, calling over his shoulder. "It's okay, Peter. Here's Mummy."

"Mommy! Mommy! Come and watch!" He hadn't sounded this animated since the virus struck.

It wasn't so great a present, but it sounded exactly the right chord. A small, battery operated car, bought in Hong Kong, which turned a somersault and changed direction whenever it encountered an obstruction. Peter, discovering this feature, created an obstacle course for it in the center of the room. Even his feet added to the impediments to be met. The little vehicle was somersaulting as if there were no tomorrow.

"Punkin, aren't you lucky. Did you say thank you to Ben?"

The child turned shyly. "Thank you," he murmured,

but he smiled at the same time, and that was worth more than the words. In fact, Ben discovered in the last half-hour, when you disregarded the skunk who had given him life, he was an appealing little chap, with a sweet smile.

Temporarily abandoning the car the little chap turned to Leigh. "Mommy, he called me Peter."

She, too, had registered this particular point of progress. "Well, that's your name."

Peter fiddled with the fabric of her jeans. "But he always calls me Kiddo."

"So?"

Peter still held onto her jeans as if they were a lifeline. He looked at Ben from under his lashes. "But I want him to call me Kiddo."

Leigh didn't look at Ben. She sensed that sometime, during her absence, a truce had been drawn up between the warring factions. "Then ask him, Punkin, if that's what you prefer."

Only eight feet separated them, but it might have been Lake Washington. Peter, twisting his fingers, advanced within range. "I want you to call me Kiddo. Please."

"Of course, Kiddo, whatever you like," Ben replied gently.

And feeling as if he had weathered a crisis of some magnitude, he picked the child up and tossed him into the air in the way which always thrilled his nieces. Then he caught the little boy in a great bear hug of affection. Peter squealed with muffled delight, and over his head the eyes of the adults met in unvoiced recognition.

And, loving Leigh, it wasn't hard at all.

Sixteen

*B*en reached across the table for the wine bottle. He refilled Leigh's glass, then his own. "Tell me about the visit to the in-laws."

They were eating pizza, and drinking an Australian white burgundy which Ben produced. The early evening had developed into a comfortable occasion with a distinct flavor of 'family.' There was a great deal less tension, from which they all benefited. Ben played bumper cars with Peter, read to him and did some of the silly things which entertained his nieces for hours. Delighted by this form of treatment Peter blossomed, giggled, sought Ben out. Not once did he pout or cling to Leigh.

"It went pretty well." Leigh halved a segment of pizza for her son. "They were delighted to see Peter, and you had a good time, too, didn't you Punkin, with Gramps and Gramma?"

Peter turned to Ben. "They've got a swing in their yard, and a pool. I'm learning to swim."

"With 'floaties' you sure are!" She took Ben's plate, unloading the last segment onto it and tossing in some salad for good measure.

With interjections from Peter she described for Ben the remarkable house on the Heights, overlooking the Bay. How sad really, all the trappings of a successful life, made suddenly poorer when there was no longer an immediate heir.

"And in a way it was a bit of a victory, this visit. I felt that my father-in-law respected me more because I'd refused to submit to his decrees. In fact, I guess there was mutual respect. Really, Pete's accident meant a great loss to them. You have to remember, they lost this wonderful son who could do no wrong. And there was one moment when my heart went out to the old man. He took me away from the house and asked me, in a gruff, embarrassed way, if I'd be prepared to keep all the sordid details about the Malibu apartment and those other, unexplained items to myself. Not to tell his wife, Doris. She has no understanding at all of her son's real nature. Isn't that a bit pathetic?"

"It suggests to me that he recognizes you were also a victim. As I've been saying forever."

"Perhaps. But you know, I do feel that I've achieved something really worthwhile. It's not just this place to live in instead of the dump, and my own car again, after all these months. It's not even the financial aspect, although that's vital, but the knowledge that I fought by myself for what I knew to be right. And actually won."

Ben grinned at her. "Didn't I always say you were a

feisty dame?" Then he added, "Did you tell them about me?"

"What was there to tell? There's this Australian pilot who's very stubborn and can't take no for an answer?"

"Sounds okay to me. You could have added, 'And I'm going to marry him. Next year.' "

Leigh, suddenly very still, said quietly, "But I'm not. That's your version of the facts, not mine. I'm simply prepared to let you hang around to move the furniture."

■ ■ ■

Ben read 'Thomas the Tank Engine Meets Henry,' when Peter was ready for bed. There is always something delicious about newly bathed small children; a smell which is the combination of moist skin and soap. Peter's hair clung to his brow and the nape of his neck in damp, black spikes. He listened to the story of Henry, who was very haughty, and Thomas, who was very humble, with great seriousness. Ben was allowed to tuck him into bed and kiss him goodnight.

"You'd better watch out," he warned Leigh when he emerged from the night-time ritual. "You're going to be a pretty poor substitute when I'm gone."

Leigh was stacking the dishwasher and tidying the table. "I'll risk it." She began to measure out ground coffee.

Suddenly, without the chaperonage of Peter, the atmosphere became more charged. Ben followed her into the kitchen and watched her get down two mugs and find the creamer. Neither of them took milk, so they had no need for that, nor for the spoons which followed onto the tray.

"Leigh." He took her head in his hands, turning her towards him, looking down at her in a manner which made her bones feel rubbery.

"Oh, Ben, don't." She might not have wasted her breath. The desire was like a rawness in his eyes. Still holding her face he kissed her in a way which was entirely new. If ever a kiss asked a question, this one did. Her back was pinned against the door, his body pressed against hers, thigh against thigh, ribcage against ribcage with her hands crushed between. She was aware of taut muscles and a hardness down the length of him. There was an immediacy which was at total variance with the easy-going Ben who teased her and comforted her and listened to her confessions. And it was far more threatening.

Was this pay-up time? Was this the next, obvious step which he would demand? The moment of metamorphosis, when the companion with whom she was comfortable became the intransigent Man of Steel, and discovered just how inadequate she was?

Panic overwhelmed her like an incoming tide. She tried to close her mouth, but Ben's tongue continued to intrude, not roughly or invasively, but with a persistence that fed the panic. She wrenched her head away.

"What's wrong?"

"I . . . I . . . the coffee's ready."

He didn't try to capture her head again. "A kiss is not a rape, you know. It's an invitation. A trial, shall we say, to find out if the chemistry's right."

"Yes, I know. I . . . perhaps the chemistry's wrong."

"You know that's not true." He released her, then turned to pick up the tray. "Come on, my darling." His voice was matter of fact and held none of the husky passion of a moment ago. "This is clearly time for coffee and more True Confessions."

"You're not mad?"

"Never with you, honey. Sad, frustrated half to death, but not mad."

She gulped. "But who's doing the confessing? I have nothing else to tell you. Or are you going to confess to me?" And she smiled slightly at the thought.

Ben set the tray down on the coffee table and poured them both mugfuls. "This is again Uncle Ben, your Father Confessor, in action. And you're going to explain to me what it is about sex that you find so scary."

He made her sit by him on the couch, cuddled her against him. This time there was no threat, just comfort.

"I can't tell you, because I don't know."

"Have you always hated the thought of sex? Even when you were a kid? Did your mother tell you it was bad news; that nice girls always said No, or something?"

"Of course she did. That goes without saying, but I didn't believe her. It was the same kind of thing that went out the window with the Tooth Fairy and Santa Claus."

What was it about Ben that encouraged her to open up? Even to Nancy she'd never as much as touched upon this most private of her terrors. But Ben managed to unlock floodgates of which she was only vaguely aware.

"Go on." He let his fingers play with her ear, gently wandering across the nape of her neck.

Even so, even with his support, it was hard getting started. Like looking for ghosts under the bed when she was a girl.

She took a deep breath. "When we first met, Pete and I, it was all okay. I felt the way most girls feel, had the usual charge of hormones, the usual appetites. But once we were married everything changed. It was quite gradual. Not an overnight thing, you understand. His love making changed. He demanded more, things I hated to do but he said were normal between people who loved each other. As far as I could see they all revolved round my humiliation. But when the person you imagine you're in love with says, 'this is something you'll enjoy, because you love me,' and you're actually detesting it, you begin to lose faith in yourself."

"So that was the start. Pete and his perversions."

"I didn't say they were perversions."

"You didn't have to. It's just another hedge, I s'pose."

Leigh turning her head within the crescent of his arm. "What do you mean, another hedge?"

"Something Jane said." He wished he hadn't introduced that. Leigh might find his discussing her with Jane as irritating as he found the wretched Nancy. And she'd be sure to have a tough time understanding the analogy of Sleeping Beauty. He dropped a kiss on her neat cap of hair. "I didn't mention that we have her blessing, did I? Her actual words were, 'I'd adore to have Leigh as a sister-in-law.'"

"Ben, you can't say that. It's against the rules. My rules. How can you tell such a whopping fib when there's weeks and weeks until the February date? And then I shall be sending you on your way. In fact, anybody with half an ounce of brains would have done so already."

He continued to stroke her hair, watching her profile as she buried her nose in the coffee mug, as if seeking refuge in there. "Can you tell me the sort of thing Pete expected you to do? Or is it too painful?"

"I don't think I can. I buried it all with Pete." She wasn't sure if his sigh was genuine or play-acting.

"Then we'll just pretend we're back at the beginning again. A first date, very chaste. A bit of necking. No more until you're ready, I promise."

"Really promise? You'll not get mad?"

Ben thought sadly how much she gave away with those

words. He didn't have to know the things Pete had forced upon her, because his imagination told enough. No wonder the lovely smile had vanished. What was it like, waiting each night for someone who would demand that you perform humiliating acts in the name of love? Someone who'd probably enjoyed himself already with this or that girlfriend, in the Malibu apartment, some hotel room; and who saw the trivial matter of sex with his wife more as a means of keeping her in line? Certainly not a sharing of their love.

Had Pete ever actually loved her? Even at the beginning? Or did he see her as a suitably tactile girl, the sort he could mold to his taste? After all, he'd been in the sack with that blond sheila at the engagement party.

"Cuddle up. Keep close."

Leigh obeyed, letting her body melt against his, her head nestling in the gap between shoulder and chin.

"Nice?"

"Mmm."

"There, you see. That's the first time you've really trusted me to do as I promise. A milestone day, in more ways than one."

Allowing all the tautness to leave her body Leigh said, "That's the other thing I meant to say. Thank you for being so nice to Punkin."

"No problem. You've got a great kid there."

■ ■ ■

A long time later Ben said, "Bed, honey. Another crack of dawn start. That's the price we men of action pay."

Leigh was nearly asleep. She raised her head and Ben kissed her very gently. No urgency, no threat.

"You're a very sweet person, Ben Beresford. There was

no need to do that."

Ben, thinking of the old tale of the snail creeping up the side of the well, replied, "My darling, perhaps I did it to make me feel better. Sleep well."

Seventeen

In the following weeks the texture and rhythm of Leigh's and Peter's lives settled down.

For a while Leigh contemplated returning to her old haunts of California, then she rejected the notion on two counts. First, although the peace pipe had been smoked with the Pendletons, the distance between them contributed to her feelings of independence. Second, she decided that too much had happened for her old friendships ever to resume their original status. And even with the child support the Pendletons were paying her, she was scarcely in their financial league.

Anyway, she liked Washington. She even liked Kirkland, now that her accommodation was improved. Kirkland had water and trees, flower beds and interesting shops. It was pretty and convenient. She'd come of age here, gained a certain respect for herself. It was fast finding a place in her affections.

Something else happened, so slowly that at first Leigh was too involved in her own affairs to notice it. Nancy was spending an increasing amount of time in Portland.

At first, as her friend's intrepid old jalopy, held together by no more than its rust, set off once more southwards down the I-5, Leigh assumed that it was connected with her mother's chronic illness. It took quite a while for the penny to drop. Nance the Misogamist, Nance the president of Emotional Addicts Anonymous, had fallen for another guy.

In some ways that was part of the cycle, too. Nancy had been her vital, emotional crutch when she was at her lowest. She would always be special and appreciated for her unwavering support, but Leigh was gathering herself together and moving on. Nancy, too, was moving on.

Another part of the cycle, and one which simply meant a few alterations. Leigh enrolled Peter into a local Pre-school; three mornings a week, starting after Christmas. Her Punkin was also finding his feet.

Ben's letters, Ben's phone calls, his occasional gifts, though rarely of much content, became an intrinsic part of the texture of Leigh's life. The spice which added flavor to each day. He would phone from wherever he was, from New Zealand, Perth, or Hong Kong, having worked out the difference and translated it all into Pacific Time. Leigh came to appreciate the sound of his voice far more than she cared to admit.

■ ■ ■

Ben called from the anonymity of his room in a luxurious Singapore hotel. "I want you to spend Christmas here. No, not here. In Sydney. Share it with me and the family. Please, Leigh?"

"Ben, I can't." The image of a summer Christmas in the land Down-under formed like a bubble above a cartoon character. "I'm committed to going to Los Altos, with the in-laws. It'll be their first Christmas without Pete, and it's going to be tough for them. Having Punkin about will help."

Ben hoped that his disappointment didn't cross the Pacific. "Yes, of course. I understand." He did some fast thinking, rearranging in his mind the wonderful trilogy of Leigh and Sydney and Christmas. "But there's a delivery scheduled for early January. Will you and Peter come then, if I can get you onto the flight?" There should be no problem with that, a 747 had over four hundred seats. Delivery flights were sometimes only half-full.

The bubble which had burst when she'd refused Christmas re-formed and floated in the air. "Ben, I can't afford plane fares anywhere, let alone Australia. The Pendletons pay me an allowance, enough to get by in comfort. Not a fortune."

"That's no problem. You leave the finance to me. Just say you'll come."

Again she hesitated, doing some calculations. Where would she be staying? At his place? What would Ben be wanting in return? Wasn't she doing more than playing with fire, to use Nancy's analogy?

Ben could read her pause as it stretched across the ocean. "Leigh, honey, no strings. I promise. You know by now that you can trust me. And you can write all the rules."

"But won't it be grossly expensive?"

"That's my concern. Just say you'll come. Please."

"But . . ." She was running out of arguments.

"Leigh, close your eyes and picture it all. The Blue Mountains all hazy in the sunshine and smelling of gum leaves, and parrots in flight. Sydney Harbor in summer. There's a pool on our point. Peter will be swimming before you get home. Jane says she's dying to see you again, and you'll be able to meet Janna and Millie. And there are two bedrooms in my place. You and Peter can have your own room. Say you'll come?"

"It does sound inviting." It might be nice to enjoy a bit of sunshine in January.

"Fantastic." She could hear his pleasure. "You'll not regret it, I promise."

As she replaced the phone some minutes later Leigh wondered if that was true. Wasn't she simply making the inevitable parting, on the twenty-first of February, all the more difficult to contemplate? Wasn't she going to pay the price of an Australian vacation a thousand-fold?

She would cross that bridge when she came to it, she resolved. And nobody could accuse her of leading Ben on. She'd been totally honest with him. Never had she even hinted at their sharing a long term commitment.

Of course, there was one small dishonesty. A sin of omission, when you thought of it. She'd never actually told him that she loved him. But then, she'd refused to acknowledge that particular fact even to herself.

■ ■ ■

Christmas at the Pendleton mansion followed the familiar pattern of previous years. Only this year there was no Pete to play golf with his father or to relate to his admiring mother the small and large accounts of his professional achievements. In Pete's repertoire there was an unending supply of such anecdotes, all calculated to impress his audience. And nobody was ever more impressed than his adoring mother.

Paula, Pete's sister, and her husband, Howard, always shared the Heights' Christmas, along with their daughter. Chelsea was a confidant young lady, poised on the brink of adolescence. Without having a great deal in common, Leigh and Paula always got along well enough. Chelsea, however, was a blessing. She adored her cousin now he was almost four and had sufficient sense to take an interest in things. She took upon herself his entertainment like one with a mission.

The festivities followed the traditional form. The usual overabundance of food and alcohol and the lavishness of the decorations. A tree of twenty feet dominated the vast entrance vestibule, the lamps of which could have lit a small town. The only difference was the genuine attempt of her mother-in-law to make everything seem as it had been before the accident. None-the-less, two small incidents found a place in Leigh's memory.

The first moment was on Christmas Day. The seven of them gathered in the dining room, only one leaf in a table which could, at full stretch, seat twenty. On the sideboard there stood in splendor a haunch of beef, a ham of gargantuan proportions, a turkey with all the trimmings. Such fare, Leigh thought, could have fed all Ethiopia for a week, herself and her son for years.

Peter Sandford Pendleton Senior, he who had bought his first rundown apartment block in a less salubrious quarter of Haight-Ashbury back in the fifties and from those humble beginnings forged for himself a slice of the Good

Life, cleared his throat and looked round his assembled family. "I'd like to say a grace. Shall we all hold hands?"

When the human link was formed he continued, "Before we begin our meal I want us to take a few minutes to remember someone who isn't here today. Someone who was a very special son, and brother, a very special husband and father . . ."

The silence was painful. Leigh knew without looking that Doris was weeping, the tears spilling uncontrolled over her carefully made-up cheeks. She found there was quite a sizable lump in her throat, too. Not because she missed Pete for one second. The irony of it was that if he had not died she and her punkin would not be seated at this table today. Had he lived she knew with certainty they would at this moment be in the middle of a painful, messy and probably grossly public divorce case

The tears which pricked behind her lids were not for Pete. They were for two other people, just as dead. For the innocent, eager girl who had so willingly offered herself to him, and for the person he might have been, and Doris fondly imagined he was.

But Pete was dead. No good would come from raking over the coals. It was better that his mother keep her proud memories intact and unsullied.

Leigh was seated between Howard, to her left, and Peter perched to her right. His high chair allowed him to sit easily at the adult table. In her effort to contain the threatening tears, the tears of regret, Leigh squeezed the two hands with which she was linked harder than she'd intended, and Peter said indignantly, "Ow! You hurt me."

The moment was over.

"Right!" The old man blinked quickly, and finished the grace. "Who's for some of this beef?"

■ ■ ■

The second moment took place the following day. Chelsea was, as usual, entertaining Peter. She had created a den for him under the table of what was officially entitled the Morning Room because it faced east. It was in fact the smaller and more comfortable of the two living rooms.

Paula and Leigh were well into their second cups of coffee and supervising in a casual way.

"There's something I wanted to ask you," Paula began. She was an elegant, confident young woman in her early thirties, very like Pete in appearance. She was secure in her marriage, herself and her place in society. Money, plenty of it, seemed to help on all those points.

Leigh wasn't too sure how much or how little Paula knew about the squabble for Peter which had been resolved so recently. Paula's next words informed her. "And something I have to say. We wanted to congratulate you, Howard and I. We were impressed with the way you stood up to Daddy like that, refusing to give up Peter. When I heard that he'd filed in court for custody I was shocked, and told him exactly how I felt. I guess it must have been motivated by grief. "

"So I get one gold star?"

Paula smiled. "At least two, in my estimation, and I'm sure Daddy respects you for your stand. But that's not what I wanted to say, really. It's a bit hard, to be honest, because I don't want to sound disloyal."

Leigh noticed the way Paula was fiddling with her rings in small, tight movements. "Don't worry. I won't broadcast what you tell me."

Paula lowered her voice, although there was scant need because the cousins were busily involved arranging cushions and throw blankets to form a satisfactory interior to their house. "It's about Pete. As I said, it's hard to find the right words, but how was he, how did you find him, as a husband?"

"What can I say? He was okay. Always generous with money, anyway."

"Other people's money?"

"So you know that, too."

"Not entirely. To be honest it's more conjecture on Howard's part. But that's nobody's business but yours and Daddy's. No, I was meaning in other ways. You see, I sometimes thought when he was a kid that he wasn't quite normal. I know it's not the authorized version according to the parents, but for myself I was bothered about some of the things he did. Sadistic things."

Leigh was instantly alert. "What sort of sadistic things?"

"They often involved me, or if not me personally, my possessions. Anything that was precious to me, like dolls or some new article of clothing. And he was so clever at covering up his tracks it was hard to pinpoint the blame. But the worst, I suppose, was the kitten."

"Tell me."

Paula made an uncharacteristically awkward movement of brushing her hair, black and glossy and so like Pete's, away from her brow. "I'd wanted this kitten for ages. There were all sorts of objections about Pete being allergic. When I was about eight or nine, and Pete was about eleven, I finally got my kitten. The cutest little thing, all gray, which with great originality I called Smoke. I adored her. Pete ignored her presence for some time, or certainly did in my presence. Then he resorted to no more than the odd, irritating tail tweak or toe in the ribs if he thought he was unobserved. But, when Smoke was about three or four months old, we found her outside on the driveway with her back broken. And we had to have her put to sleep.

"Nobody knew anything until the gardener came the next week. He asked me in rather an odd way how the kitty was and I told him about the accident. He said, 'That was no accident. You go ask your big brother.' He looked kind of knowing.

"So I did. The brouhaha which followed was unbelievable. At first Pete vowed that the gardener was making it all up. But finally he confessed that he'd dropped Smoke out of the window to see it she could land on all four feet. But not the first floor, nor the second. He'd gone up to the maids' quarters on the third floor for his little experiment."

"That's disgusting," Leigh said quietly. But she wasn't altogether surprised.

Paula, still turning her rings in fussy little circles, avoided Leigh's eyes. "That was one of so many incidents; to me it was the worst. But Mamma took me aside and explained that I shouldn't tell anyone. The honor of the family, etc. etc. I remember screaming that he was a monster and should be locked up.

"But he grew up to be so charming. You know how he could wrap people round his little finger, how he seemed to be surrounded by a halo of charisma. He was such fun, such good company. So I told myself that they were exactly what Mamma said, boyish pranks. Part of the past. It was only when I was telling Howard about it all that I began to wonder again. Does that side of a person really disappear, is it outgrown, or does it stay an intrinsic part of the personality?"

Leigh felt closer to her sister-in-law than she had in all the years of knowing her. These disclosures showed a another side of the sophisticated young woman hitherto never suspected.

There'd been a fraction of time, while she told the tale of Smoke, when Leigh was tempted to protest, 'Why didn't you tell me all this? Before we were engaged, before we were married. Shouldn't I have known?' but the temptation only half-formed. Who, in her right mind, was going to take aside a young, besotted girlfriend, and expect to be believed? Come to that, just what words would you use? And they did say, with ample evidence to prove it, that love was blind. Back then she'd probably have attributed such a warning to jealousy on Paula's part. She'd never have listened.

"It doesn't disappear," she said quietly. "It just changes form. People instead of kittens. But Paula?"

"Yes?"

"Let's keep it your secret and mine. Howard's too, if you must. No need for Doris to know. Telling her won't change things."

Paula leaned across and squeezed her hand warmly. "Your secret and mine," she repeated, and smiled.

Eighteen

A car, arranged by Ben, came to collect Leigh and Peter. It was an ordinary, blue car with the prescribed number of wheels and other car parts, and a very ordinary, perfectly pleasant driver behind the wheel.

To Leigh it might as well have been a rough, wooden cart about to carry her up Boot Hill, to a lynch mob and a scaffold. Amazement at herself for having agreed to this fantastic flight had been succeeded by waves of panic and utter disbelief. She was, she realized, as nutty as a fruitcake. But she had promised, and there was no going back.

At SeaTac Airport the driver took care of their bags and directed them to one of the lounges set aside for second string VIPs. Again arranged by Ben.

"Mrs. Pendleton? Ben asked me to take care of you. Do

you remember me? Paddy O'Hare. We met at the last Delivery Banquet. Ben used to fly with me."

Leigh turned and smiled, relieved to find a familiar face. "Of course I remember you, Captain O'Hare. Are you in charge of today's flight?"

"For my sins." He squatted down beside Peter, who was watching him with wide-eyed interest. "And I know who you are, you're Peter."

The child accepted this easy introduction. "You wear a hat like Ben. With little wings."

"Can you say 'hi,' Punkin?"

"Hi," Peter said politely, then continued, "Ben wears a hat like that, with those things on it. We're going in a plane to visit him," and added, as an important postscript, "In 'Stralia."

"You certainly are, fella, as long as I get all the sums right." Captain O'Hare smiled and turned back to Leigh. "I must felicitate you. I was delighted to hear of your engagement."

"My . . . engagement? Oh. . . thank you."

She'd been going to say 'my what?' but caution sprang to her rescue. Had it been necessary for Ben to pretend a formal connection in order to get her onto this flight? Were delivery flights with TransOz the exclusive preserve of families and VIPs? She had no idea, of course, but she was certainly not about to betray Ben.

■ ■ ■

The first class section of the plane appeared to be devoted exclusively to bigwigs of the aviation world. Power, thinly disguised behind immaculate worsted and bifocals. Leigh and Peter were in the Club section immediately aft.

Everything spoke of bandbox newness. Not a scratch, not a scuff mark in sight. Their seats were wide and comfortable. Leigh, sipping a juice and nibbling at cashew nuts, admired the choice of interior design selected by TransOz. The gum leaves theme so distinctive on the tail of each plane was carried indoors and continued in the colors of the seating and panels, and in the uniforms of the flight attendants. Cool colors, soft greens and earthy browns, with just a hint of the pastel gum blossoms. They were the hues, she imagined, of the Australian bush.

The service was impeccable. Before they left the ground Peter was given a bag containing crayons and coloring papers, toys and games. The games were a little ambitious, but Peter was delighted by such personal attention. And so much TLC was delightfully soothing. Aware that she'd already burned her bridges, Leigh put her anxieties on hold and settled back to enjoy the flight.

There were so many aspects of this whole, bizarre, vacation which raised unanswered questions to contend with. There was the formidable army of Ben's nearest and dearest, the Beresford Tribe. Would they all be seeing her in the rose-tinted light of a prospective relative-in-law? What would Jane have told them? Or Ben, himself?

She knew herself to be totally inadequate when it came to family. She had vivid memories of childhood experiences, almost always tinged with green, when she'd been invited to a meal at a friend's house. She would watch the interplay between siblings, scrapping, bickering and jockeying for pole position. Sometimes the arguments would be deafening, and then, briefly, she'd be glad of her only child status. More often there was that wonderful feeling of the clan, the mutual support which combines disparate personalities into the charmed circle of a family. And she, the outsider, would envy them with all of her being.

The other major issue was the question of how they would get along, she and Peter and Ben, in the day-to-day matters of life. A three-week period to live through, filled with breakfasts and lunches, rubbing shoulders in shared space. Shared intimate space. Would Ben be away flying for part of that time? Did he expect her to be Susie Homemaker? Wash clothes and keep house? Such matters could only be resolved upon arrival. And she did trust Ben. She really did.

Always, it seemed, she struggled to fulfill other folks' perceptions of her. First, to be the ideal daughter as envisioned by her mother, which meant one ever popular, but never less than ladylike. Even teachers exacted roles for you to play out, roles which reflected their teaching abilities, their ambitions for you.

And then there was the position of wife. Pete and his impossible expectations. In retrospect, had he ever loved her at all? Even one tiny bit? Or were his professions of total adoration simply lies like all his other lies? Had he deliberately chosen a girl eight years his junior in order to mold her to his particular requirements? He was demanding, determined that she be a competent homemaker, confident and serene hostess, as well as mother to his genius child. And, maybe most important of all, sex slave.

The only person who'd always been delighted with her, without reservation, was her father, but then, hadn't he abandoned her without a backward glance?

And now Ben. How high was the pedestal he'd prepared?

She glanced down at Peter, her chaperone. With single-minded zest he was busily creating a sci-fi world within the coloring book which was part of his entertainment packet. A lurid sky of pink was fast engulfing Mickey Mouse and Minnie, with total disregard for such minor details as outlines.

"Hello there, Mrs. Pendleton! Well, well."

The voice invaded the somewhat other-worldly state into which Leigh had allowed herself to slip. It brought her senses back together with a jolt. She regarded the owner of the voice impassively as the taste of bile invaded her mouth, and her skin crawled.

"You do remember me, don't you? We met at the dinner at the Columbus Club? I'm Noeline Williams."

Leigh bit back a sharp retort. "Of course I remember you."

She wished she'd noticed her before and had time to prepare her defenses. Ben might say casually that they'd had a thing going, he and Noeline. Leigh, with her female antennae fully alerted, recognized jealousy at a thousand paces. She also recognized the signal that battle stations were being assumed. Noeline was one of the most senior of the TransOz stewardesses. Nothing short of a six-bell emergency would cause her to abandon the First Class cabin. She must have ventured among the lesser mortals only because she knew Leigh to be on board.

"And this is your little boy?" cooed Noeline.

Peter paused briefly in his vigorous scribbling to cast a casual glance over this new arrival.

"Yes, this is Peter."

"What a darling little fellow! What delightful coloring. Just like his daddy?"

"Yes," Leigh said again.

"And I gather we have an engagement to celebrate." Noeline scarcely paused to hear Leigh's responses. You could have sweetened all of Hershey's output on any given day with the sugar in her voice. "Such an exciting occasion. I was just thrilled when I heard, and Captain O'Hare too. He sent me back with this."

Leigh hadn't noticed until this moment that Noeline carried a bottle of champagne, a very expensive-looking bottle, with a gold-foiled neck and all. A second stewardess appeared from behind, bearing a tray of glasses. Having a witness meant that social politics must be obeyed.

"That's very kind of Captain O'Hare. Please thank him. But if you don't mind, I'd rather not open it right now."

"Oh, but you must," Noeline insisted.

"To be frank I don't feel like alcohol right now, but it looks like wonderful champagne. I'm sure Captain O'Hare will understand. I'd rather keep it."

"No, no. We're all absolutely dying to drink your health," Noeline bulldozed on, refusing to accept Leigh's response. "I hope you'll not deny us that little pleasure. We absolutely adore Ben, you see. He's a favorite with all the stewardesses. Isn't that so, Heather?"

"Oh, gosh. Yes." Heather replied in the tone of one who would rather be anywhere else.

Leigh was controlling her irritation by sheer willpower. "Then be my guests. By all means drink a toast, but count me out."

The annoyance oozing from every pore only acted as encouragement to Noeline. The cork burst from the bottle with the report of a starter's pistol, making several surprised passengers jump in their seats. A cataract of Australia's best vintage champagne cascaded over Leigh's shoulder and trickled into a pool on her lap.

"Oh dear. Oh dear. How terribly careless of me." Noeline's eyes, belying the words, were bright and hard as polished agates.

There was no point in screeching, 'And isn't that what you'd intended from the start?' because it was just the response she sought. With icy deliberation Leigh ignored her.

"Peter, you wait here for a few minutes," she said with all the calmness she could muster. She turned to the now thoroughly embarrassed Heather. "Perhaps you could stay with him?"

She stood with dignity, managing to grind Noeline's foot under hers as she left the seat; pretending not to notice her sharply indrawn breath. The sticky beverage trickled down her legs as she stalked along to the stewardesses' bay between the cabins. With slow, deliberate movements she carefully sponged off the worst of the champagne, using the time to allow her fury to cool. She would not play that woman's game. She would not.

She was still toweling dry the offending areas when Noeline appeared again.

"So sorry about that," she said coolly, with no attempt at sincerity. "I'll put the bottle into the chiller. You can fetch it when we reach Sydney. Perhaps you'll be ready for something alcoholic by then." She made an officious show of refilling the drip coffee machine.

As the silence lengthened the older woman began again, on a new tack. "You should have listened to me back in Seattle, you know. I did try to warn you, that evening, but perhaps it's still not too late. After all, what's an engagement? Only a promise. Nothing binding. Right?"

"Right." Leigh returned the towel to the counter.

"I'd feel just terrible if I let you go through with this marriage without trying to warn you. Perhaps I didn't make myself plain, last time."

"You did."

"Yes, but my dear, I have a little more experience than

you, and in the course of my career I've seen a bit of the world. I can tell you that someone as jaded as Ben Beresford will have a sweet girl like you on toast for breakfast."

"You think so?"

"I think so." A melodramatic pause and a slight sigh. "I've seen so many young men like Ben. They fly to these exotic places, and they taste the forbidden fruits that can be found for a price in Jakarta and Bangkok and Hong Kong." Another little sigh. "It's hard for you to imagine, but the vice that's available is beyond description. In the light of such debauchery what hope have we decent Western girls?"

"Oh, I don't know," Leigh countered. She was ready to return to her seat but fury rendered her legs immobile. How did this woman have the gall to utter such garbage?

"Believe me." Noeline patted Leigh a little awkwardly on the shoulder. Clearly this was a new role for her, still requiring practice.

Leigh shrugged the hand impatiently away. Then she felt her anger cooling, changing to pity. Noeline, she realized, was a person who has never found it necessary to develop niceness of personality as an alternative to beauty. "You don't know what I like, Noeline." She tried to keep her voice kind. "And after all, you did have your chance, so maybe you don't know what Ben likes, either? Let's leave it at that."

Noeline regarded her with the chill of permafrost. "You don't deserve my help."

"I didn't ask for it," Leigh replied crisply.

■ ■ ■

"Sorry about all that," Heather apologized when Leigh returned to her seat. "I know she can be a bitch, at times.

We all dread the rough side of her tongue."

Leigh felt about a foot taller. After all, another battle had been fought, and she'd emerged the winner. "Don't be," she replied. "It probably sounds dumb, but I actually enjoyed it, crossing swords with such a pro. And thanks for keeping Punkin company."

"We did okay, didn't we, Peter? But Noeline was right about one thing. We all do like Ben, and we hope you'll be very happy," Heather continued. She had an open, cheerful face and a pleasant manner. "Actually, I was on my way to you with a message from Captain O'Hare, when Noeline collared me. He wondered if you and Peter would like to come up and visit the cockpit?"

Nineteen

*I*n a perfect world the adrenaline flow released by her duel with Noeline should have sustained Leigh for some time. Peter slept across a large chunk of the Pacific, which helped, and when they arrived Paddy O'Hare efficiently eased her path through the necessary formalities. Despite all this, her stomach was once again in knots of anxiety before they cleared Immigration. Finally they emerged from the Customs area to be confronted by a sea of unknown, eager faces and a babble of excited voices.

And then, amidst the hubbub, there was Ben. Not, as she'd feared in that unrestful semi-doze which passes for sleep aboard a plane, at the head of a monstrous Welcoming Party. He was alone, looking tanned and healthy, his hair more sun-bleached than ever. He was wearing jeans and a faded blue shirt which matched the color of his eyes. He was more welcome than the discovery of long-sought treasure.

"Ahoy, there, Leigh! Kiddo!"

"Mommy, it's Ben. I can see Ben."

Peter abandoned her with the baggage trolley and ran towards the outstretched arms. He was seized, tossed, gathered to Ben's chest. It was the usual ritual; but over his head Ben's eyes sought Leigh's, conveying a message of sheer delight that she was actually there, standing on the soil of his native land.

Suddenly she found herself blushing and at a loss for words. Thank heavens for Peter, who kept up a stream of excited chatter. They walked out into the bright sunshine of Sydney on an early January morning, and towards Ben's car.

"I flied the plane, Ben. I sat in the seat and that man put big things on my ears. And people talked in my ears. And Mommy too. We sat in the cock . . . in the cock . . ."

"In the cockpit."

"Yes, in there. And the man said he knowed you. And the lady threw fizzy pop all over Mommy. She had to clean it all off. And we drank juice and I ate meat balls . . . and . . . and . . ."

"Steady." Ben was amused by his enthusiasm. "So you enjoyed flying the plane. But what's this about fizzy stuff all over Mummy?"

Leigh replied. "It was nothing, Ben. An accident, no more." They were at the start of this vacation. Nothing was going to upset the applecart, least of all Noeline Williams.

■ ■ ■

Ben had put considerable thought into this entire project, which he saw as a make or break event. For the first and only time he would have a home field advantage. Leigh would be removed from what he saw as the subversive influence of Wicked Witch Nancy, and, with a little luck to support his effort, he hoped to sway her in his direction. At least give her time to learn the meaning of trust.

In order to cover all bases he'd sought advice of the three women within the family circle, his mother and the wives of his brothers. So it was that the car awaiting them in the car park area was not his usual Mercedes convertible, but instead a sensible Ford sedan, with a sensible car seat secured in the rear for Peter.

He was pleased that Sydney, whose January weather could be fickle, had seen fit to turn on a real beauty of a day. Even when viewed through less partial eyes, the place looked lovely.

"We live on the North Shore," he explained as they drove along a wide boulevard which bordered parkland. The skyline of the city loomed ahead of them. "Across the bridge. This area's called Kings Cross. Not the safest place to be at night, but there are smashing little bistros and nightclubs. If you look across to the right you'll see the Opera House come into view at any minute."

They edged their way into the slowly moving stream of traffic approaching the great arch of the Harbor Bridge. Then they were on it, and there below was the staggeringly lovely stretch of water which is Sydney Harbor, dotted even at this early hour with ferries and small craft.

"Those little launches buzzing about like busy insects? They're water taxis. We might take one, and have lunch at Doyle's, down the harbor. Would you like that, Kiddo? The best fish and chips in the world!"

Peter pointed at a larger craft reversing out from quay. "I want to go in that boat."

"You probably will. That's one of the ferries which comes to Cremorne." Ben indicated to the right as he replied. "The point of land jutting out down there is Kirribilli, where the Prime Minister stays. My place is one point more easterly, in Cremorne. My parents live further across, in the next suburb."

Leigh could see why he'd compared the city with Seattle, but she could see where the comparison ended abruptly, too. It had something to do with the quality of light. Even in California she couldn't recall light as sharp, as clear as this was. It gave everything an added brilliance.

They left the expressway and the road began to wind, following the contours of the harbor bays. It was all very leafy and pretty but, even to her inexperienced eye, pretty expensive.

"Here we are." Ben drew the car into a car port and opened the trunk to unload their bags. The house was large, dignified and elderly, but nicely painted. It stood to the west of the promontory of land which jutted into the harbor. It was a little above its immediate neighbors, and surrounded by a long established garden of shrubs and flowering trees which were a riot of summer scents and color.

They crossed to the house by a deck which traversed the gap from the road. Peter was immensely impressed by a house which was entered by way of a bridge. He tested it out several times in the interval it took the adults to follow him.

"This place used to belong to my grandparents," Ben explained. "Mum grew up here. After our grandfather's death the old girl had it divided into two, because it was far too big for her alone. That's when she put in this deck, as access to the top floor. When she died she left the property in equal parts to we three boys and our mother. I bought out Mum's quarter, so now I own the top half. A married couple rents the lower floor from Dave and John."

He unlocked the door, standing aside to let Leigh precede him into the wide, open living room. Peter skipped ahead, still bubbling with the excitement of everything.

"Oh, Ben. This is a lovely place."

He hoped he didn't sound too smug. "I'm glad you like it."

The living room had been created by a fairly rigorous removal of walls, and given an abundance of light by building a wide picture window into the wall facing the harbor. The floors were all polished wood which had gathered a darkness and richness over the years, with scattered rugs of soft, attractive colors. The furniture was a mixture of elegant antiques and sensible, comfortable rattan topped by an assortment of squidgy cushions.

There was a bowl of fruit on the coffee table and, a delightful postscript which touched her heart, a somewhat clumsily arranged cluster of flowers on the dining table.

Peter raced to the wide window and scrambled onto the padded cushions of the built-in seat. "Mommy, come and look. Come and see the boat."

"In one minute, Punkin. Let me put this stuff down."

"I'll show you your room," Ben said. "In here. You have your own bathroom through there." He preceded her into a bedroom of pleasant proportions, furnished with twin beds over which were spread linen covers of cream and fawn. "Hanging space, drawers, all that stuff. If you need anything else you have only to say."

He set down the two suitcases he was carrying and put an arm round her shoulders, drawing her close. "Welcome to Australia, my darling," he said quietly, smiling down into her eyes; and kissed her very gently.

"Mommy," Peter called insistently. "You said you'd come and see."

Ben released her. "I'll get coffee started, and breakfast. You'll have eaten on the plane, I know, at some ungodly hour, but I was up before six to get to the airport, and I'm famished."

▪ ▪ ▪

The view from the wide picture window was spectacular. Beyond the deck, over the tops of the frangipani trees and the tiled roofs of a scattering of other houses, lay the waters of the harbor, dancing and sparkling in the morning light. There was a small island with some sort of fortification on it. Beyond that, to the west, the unmistakable sail-roofs of the Opera House.

A large craft was making its way up the harbor from the entrance. It was a very ungainly craft, all superstructure, and it was this which had gained Peter's attention. Leigh sat herself down on the padded seat beside him and watched the ship's stately progress. The harbor was alive with activity. Would she ever become bored with a view like this?

"A container ship," Ben called from the kitchen, which was separated from the living room only by breakfast bar. A delicious smell of sizzling bacon was starting to pervade the place. "Probably cars, from Japan. And the smaller boats which are green, yellow and red, they're the suburban ferries, taking commuters to work in the city."

"It's magnificent." Leigh thought how trite and inadequate that sounded. But what other words would be more appropriate, when one was facing a million dollar view like the one spread before her? Very nice?

"Food's on the table," Ben said. "And coffee. Even if you're not hungry you can come and watch the lions feed, while I fill you in on what I've got planned for us. And,

Kiddo . . . you can look in that cupboard over there, and you'll find some toys and things." He turned to Leigh. "I prevailed upon Dan. He's John's son. He had a great time finding things he thought Peter would enjoy. Bundles of cars, of course, and the odd plane, a few books and games."

Exploring such treasures would keep any small boy enthralled for the foreseeable future.

There is something about the smell of crisply fried bacon. Even though she seemed to have done nothing but eat during those long hours crossing the Pacific, Leigh found space for a couple of slices and an egg. Ben had set the table with mats and napkins and lovely, old silverware. Inherited from his grandmother?

He started to explain his carefully prepared schedule while they ate. "We're having a family get-together tomorrow night, so the others can meet you. I thought you'd be too dog-tired tonight; and, anyway, David can't get away until Saturday morning. He and Jane and the girls are spending the weekend with my parents."

"Tomorrow's Friday," Leigh pointed out.

"No, it's not. It's Saturday. You've forgotten. You crossed the International Date Line, so you lost a day. You'll regain it when you fly home."

Leigh fiddled with the rolled hem of her napkin. "I want to say something, Ben. I . . . I . . . don't want you to get the wrong idea, about me or about things, just because I'm here. It doesn't change anything. You must understand that, because I don't want you to think I'm here under false pretenses. It doesn't mean I'll be saying 'yes' in February."

Ben gave one of his more disarming grins. "You're here, aren't you? That's enough for me."

She concentrated on the napkin, aware of the danger of that grin, not meeting his eyes. "Sure, I'm here. But nobody would turn down the chance of a vacation in Australia. I may be dumb, but I'm not that dumb!"

"So?"

"So I think I ought to remind you of your promise. You said I could write the rules."

Ben gestured towards the other side of the room. "Do you see over there? That door leads to the passage, and my room. And see that sign above your door?"

Leigh followed his gesture with her eyes. The sign was printed on a scrap of cardboard, thumbtacked onto the wall. "O.O.B. What on earth?"

"Anywhere boys weren't allowed to go at my old school had a sign saying O.O.B. Out of Bounds. Taboo."

"What?"

He took her hand, demanding her attention. She could feel those two calluses, caused by hours of sailing. "Look at me, Leigh. This is an exercise in trust, remember? You are learning to trust me. And you're going to have a miserable holiday if you spend the entire time terrified that I'm going to force you into what you aren't ready for."

"Oh Ben, you know I don't think that."

"Yes, you do. I saw it in your face the minute you came through the door from Customs. In fact, you half expected that I'd leap on you, then and there. Isn't that so?"

"You talk more baloney than anyone else I know." But she smiled. He knew that the first little hurdle had been crossed.

But that reminded Leigh of another small bone of contention. "Ben, what exactly have you told your parents about me?"

"Do you mean as well as warning them about your squint and those three hundred pound love handles?"

"Besides that."

"The truth, of course, as all well brought up sons do. I told them you're the girl I want to marry. I explained you're as stubborn as they come, and then appealed for their help. I know it'll take all their delightful Aussie charm to persuade you that their youngest son isn't the womanizer you're so certain he is. Well, I didn't say that last bit, because there are certain things you don't share with your parents."

"But the TranzOz people think I'm your fiancée," Leigh persisted. "Captain O'Hare congratulated me and sent along some champagne."

Ben dismissed such quibbles. "Only a tiny stretching of the truth. About seven weeks premature. Perfectly permissible because that way I made certain you had a seat. Champagne, eh? Bully for old Paddy." He paused. "Was that the fizzy pop Peter said went all over you?"

"Yes."

She told him about the encounter with Noeline. She told the story well, because she was pleased with herself, and because Ben was a very appreciative audience. He laughed until he had to wipe the tears from his eyes.

Together with the egg and bacon, the silly notice pinned above her door, and those awkwardly arranged twigs of sweet smelling blooms, it cleared the air. Who, planning a seduction, bothered with sprigs of oleander and frangipani? Leigh, feeling warm and happy, realized that she really was going to enjoy this vacation, that in Ben she had found something far more precious to her, at this moment, than a lover.

She had found a friend.

Twenty

eigh lay in her bed in the soft, warm darkness and contemplated the day. She'd expected to fall asleep from sheer exhaustion, but there was too much to think over and to absorb. It had been a lovely day, filled with enjoyable activities. After breakfast Ben drove them to the North Head which guarded the entrance to the harbor, and they walked through the low scrub to the headland.

"Next stop Chile," Ben said, pointing towards the vast expanse of ocean stretched before them. Far below cobalt blue waves, even on this still day, tugged and pounded relentlessly at the steep sandstone cliffs which stood sentinel on either side of the narrow inlet. Although there were sturdy fences between them and the drop, Peter held tightly onto Ben's hand.

After their walk they swam in the public pool which was only a short stroll down the hill from the lovely house on Cremorne Point. The water was salty, because the pool was fed from the harbor. Protective walls kept stray sharks at a safe distance. Ben had even remembered to buy floaties for Peter, and he paid far more attention to the small boy than to his mother. Leigh was free to lie back in the water with her eyes closed, letting the wavelets wash soothingly over her, and to allow the sun to kiss her face.

And that was another aspect of Ben's consideration. Before venturing out he'd introduced them to an Australian Survival Pack, as he described it. Visions of anti-snake serum and cans of mace sprang to Leigh's mind, but this survival pack was far more basic. It consisted of sunscreen lotions, a fly repellent and lightweight, cotton hats for both the Pendletons.

"This is your sunburn protection gear," Ben explained. "It's to do with the combination of our sunshine and fair skins; and we can't have you breaking out in skin cancer twenty years down the road, can we? Look, Kiddo, you'll see all the Aussie kids wearing this."

He took some zinc cream, colored in lurid pink and green, and smeared it in careful stripes across Peter's cheekbones and the bridge of his button nose. "I do this, every time I go sailing. The sun off the water can fry you to a crisp. Go see yourself in the mirror. You look like an Indian brave."

After lunch they stretched out on the lawn in the dappled shade of the frangipani trees, and talked and snoozed and talked some more.

"Tell me about your Christmas," Ben said. "How did it all go, at the Heights?"

"Okay. We muddled through. But you'd think they

were laying in provisions for a siege, the quantity of food that Doris has the housekeeper prepare. It boggles the mind." She paused briefly, as she recalled her talk with Paula; but firmly rejected it. "I was there only three days. Then we went on to visit my mom."

Ben, wearing the briefest shorts she'd ever seen, and displaying more length of muscular brown thigh than seemed possible, was stretched out on an ancient, checked blanket. He propped himself up on one elbow. "That must have been fun. Was your mother's friend there?"

"No, thank heavens. He went to visit his folks. The trip no doubt financed by my mom. They live in England, I think. But we did have the pleasure of Pookie, of course, busily being psychotic and yapping his stupid head off whenever we put in an appearance. And, oh Ben . . . "

"Yes?"

"Just guess what she gave Peter for Christmas."

"Spare my dwindling little gray cells. What?"

"A bicycle. And the last thing in State of the Art, at that."

"Very thoughtful. He'll enjoy it."

"Sure," Leigh said scornfully, "When he's eight or nine. Right now all he can do is look at it in wonder. It's suitable for a fifth or sixth grader. I did hoist him onto the seat and push him about a bit, until Mom pointed out ever so gently that we were indenting the carpet, and the maid would have to vacuum again to raise the pile. There's a ten inch gap between his feet and the pedals."

Ben said thoughtfully, "I shall enjoy meeting my mother-in-law. She sounds just my sort."

"Ben."

He squinted up at her. "What's your problem?" She could recognize his desire to tease in the wickedness of his grin and the light in his eyes.

"You know what's wrong. You're stretching the rules."

■ ■ ■

It was marvelously still in the garden. Peaceful and private. There were the summer sounds of singing cicadas and chirrupy small birds, distant traffic, the muffled noises of ferries chugging importantly round the point, en route to Mossman. But in the late afternoon the peace was interrupted by a flock of shrill birds flying rapidly overhead. They sounded like noisily squabbling children as they came to perch on the eucalypt branches. Their screaming woke Leigh from her snooze.

"Rainbow lorikeets," Ben explained. "My grandmother used to feed them each afternoon. I'm often away, and pretty forgetful to boot, but they always live in hope."

He disappeared into a garden shed and returned with sunflower seed which he scattered into a wide, metal saucer. This, in turn, he raised by rope until it was suspended about eight feet above the ground. It took the lorikeets no more than half a minute to discover the feast. Then the metal disc was covered by a vivid blur of feathers, scarlet and yellow and blue, as a dozen small parrots jostled and quarreled for their supper. Ten minutes later, with a whirring of wings and a final scream for good measure, they rose as one and continued on their way.

And that wasn't the end of the enchantment. A sulphur crested cockatoo saw fit to honor them with its presence, too, sitting on a low branch and regarding them with bright, intelligent eyes. Leigh held her breath in delight at the beauty of the bird's gleaming white feathers and spiky yellow crest.

Nothing marred the evening. They barbecued outside. Ben cooked them shrimp and chicken drumsticks, and cobbled together a tossed salad. She was introduced to the couple who lived downstairs. After Peter was in bed Ben produced an ancient, battered game of Scrabble and they played that, squabbling like the lorikeets over the spelling, American versus Australian. For one who professed himself a dunce at language Ben, it turned out, was no easy conquest.

Finally her yawns could not be ignored. "Bed," Ben ordered.

Now came the crunch. But if she'd expected at least a bit of tension she was to be disappointed. The prince knew exactly what was expected of him. He held her shoulders as he kissed her gently, without even a hint of passion. "Sleep well, Leigh. I'm glad you trusted me and came to Sydney."

"Thank you, Ben, and goodnight." She was relieved and a shade disappointed at the same time. And yet, what would she have done, had he chosen to ignite a sexual flame? "It's been a fantastic day. You've made us feel very welcome."

■ ■ ■

As she prepared bedrooms and the guest bathroom for David's family Anne Beresford did quite a bit of conjecturing about this American girl, the one she would be meeting later in the day. Ben's new love.

She'd never considered his choices to be in very good taste. In the past his women had veered towards the exotic, and, in her eyes, the somewhat overblown; usually rather blousy. The only attribute they all seemed to share was a generous allowance of bulges, all in the right places. But then how could one gauge the sexual preferences of one's sons?

It was generally accepted that girls sought in their mates substitute fathers. Could the same be said for boys? It was a point worth considering. And if such was the case, in what peculiar light did her sons regard her? Never, within her understanding, did brothers wed such disparate women as John's and David's choice of wives. Or had they each latched onto a different facet of their mother's personality and selected girls who reflected that particular aspect? It would be nice to think such was the case.

There was David's Jane, dear, much loved Jane, with a behind like the rear end of a battleship and an intelligence quotient which made Mensa requirements seem puny. It would be pleasant to think that even from an early age David respected his mother's intelligence.

But there, in sharp contrast, was Barbie, married to John. The mother of his children. And the kindest adjective one could fish out for Barbie was 'dim.' She probably shared her IQ with a potato, although that was being a bit unkind to the potato.

Not that the gift wrapping surrounding the vacant space between the ears wasn't of the finest quality. Barbie was certainly a beauty, by any standards, and her body might have been the original model for the doll which was her namesake. And, to be fair, she was a competent housekeeper and mother. The children might wear fashions which their grandmother considered wildly unsuitable, but they were always tidy and mostly well behaved.

What especial aspect of his mother did John seek in his life's partner? Something decorative? Scarcely. Perhaps a smoothly run household? A mentally undemanding mate? Not quite such a flattering thought.

And now Ben's girl. If Jane were to be believed this one had him entranced. And he must think a lot of her, because part of the package was a son, soon to be four.

Well, she reflected as she put the fresh towels over the rails of the guest bathroom and checked that there was an ample supply of loo paper, time would answer all her queries.

And, after all, it was the duty of mothers to accept without criticism their children's choices.

■ ■ ■

"Do you know where we're going now?" Ben asked Peter. "We're off to the house where I lived, from when I was a tyke, even smaller than you are now. You're going to meet my Mum and Dad, and my big brothers, and their families. They have kids about the same age as you who are very excited to think they'll be able to play with you. Perhaps they'll teach you cricket."

"I don't like cricket," Peter said, hearing the word for the very first time.

"All proper boys who wear zinc on their noses like cricket," Ben replied, unruffled. "It's a very special game."

It was also very special house, the Beresford home, which Leigh was quick to recognize as it came into view. A large, Victorian structure, sitting in smooth, wide lawns and shaded by great gum trees with gnarled, twisted red trunks. A lovely house for a family. As Ben turned the car into the drive she thought of the estate in Los Altos Heights, the residence of her in-laws. This place had none of that opulence. This place, in its quiet shades of gray-green, possessed instead a subtle elegance and a sense of history. If ever one could fall in love with a collection of planks and glass, she reflected, she'd fall in love with this one.

■ ■ ■

Ben called, "Ahoy there!" and to Peter, "Watch your head, this is where we go in."

Peter was sitting high on his shoulders, finding out how giants feel, as they approached the door of the house. Leigh followed, ten steps to the rear, feeling a little like an accessory. Perhaps Ben was taking this buddy-buddy bit with Peter a bit too far. After all, wasn't she supposed to be the guest of honor? But he did wait for her to join them as they approached the porchway, and stood aside to allow her to precede them.

At that moment she experienced an overload of sensations. One might have been entering Pandemonium. They were met by the sounds of cheerful commotion interspersed with bursts of laughter, and numerous high, childish voices all seeking to have their say. It was like being enveloped in a blanket of over-bright color and noise.

From out of the group came Anne Beresford, tall and serene, blond hair escaping her somewhat careless attempt to tame it, arms outstretched. "Leigh! Welcome to Australia, my dear." She took Leigh's hand between her own and kissed her cheek. "And welcome to Peter, too."

Once the initial shock caused by sudden encounter with so many of larger-than-life personalities was past it became quite easy to identify everybody. After all, she'd a head start in being able to recognize David, scarcely changed by five years, and the parents by virtue of another generation. John was recognizable because he wore glasses like his father, and Barbie, once seen, was too unmistakably beautiful to be forgotten.

The kids were easy. Janna and Millie were familiar from photographs. Daniel, like them, was blessed with the

Beresford coloring; the shock of blond hair atop dark brows and lashes. Only young Su had been sold a little short by nature, and undoubtedly she would improve with age.

Then Jane, fifty pounds more of her than before, appeared from the general direction of the kitchen. Leigh was enveloped in a bear hug of gigantic proportions.

Jane exclaimed, "Leigh, dear! I'd not have recognized you in the street without all your lovely curls." Leigh's response was inaudible, lost in the general mass which was Jane's bosom. It was like finding harbor after a particularly turbulent ocean voyage.

The children ceased their dancing and stared expectantly at Peter. Peter, almost as overwhelmed as his mother, clung to Leigh's hand and stared back.

Anne took command. "Right, you interplanetary demons!" She addressed her grandchildren in the sort of voice which is used to being obeyed. "Anybody wanting juice and nibbles will follow me to the kitchen. Come along, Peter. You can give your mummy a break."

Leigh said gently, "Off you go, Punkin." She held her breath, praying that he would behave, not cling. But, to Peter, Anne was simply Doris Pendleton in another guise. He disappeared along the passageway with his small hand clasped in her large one, without a backward glance.

"Marvelous," said Jack Beresford, patriarch and senior partner in the highly respected General Practice of Beresford, Simmers and Beresford. "Don't get me wrong. I love 'em all dearly, but it's marvelous to be able to hear oneself think again."

He poured them drinks and asked Leigh about the state of the American dollar, and how the recent recession was affecting the economy in general, and her in particular. He was benign and fatherly, as if he had been given a role to play in a local theatrical production.

■ ■ ■

Anne was delighted with what she'd seen to date. It was abundantly apparent that Ben must have fallen hard, because Leigh was so far removed from any one of his previous women. She was a mere slip of a thing, with her short brown hair and lovely, almost mosaic eyes. And Peter was a darling little chap, too. Nicely independent, it would appear.

She sat Peter beside Millie at the kitchen table. It was one of those scrubbed pine tables round which generations of children have gathered. She produced for them the promised juice, a choice of pop or apple, and some potato chips, admonishing them, "Don't stuff yourself with these; they're emergency fare only. We'll be eating our dinner before you can say 'boo' to a goose, and there's pavlova for pudding."

Daniel said, "Num," so Peter said "Num," too. Peter was very impressed by Daniel, who, at seven, was definitely a person to be reckoned with.

"Was it fun, coming in the plane, Peter?" Anne asked, removing, as she spoke, twenty potato chips from Millie's over enthusiastic grasp.

"Yes," Peter replied, putting quite a bit of feeling into that single syllable.

"Your name's Peter. Why does your Mummy call you Punkin?" Su asked curiously.

"Cos I'm her punkin eater," Peter replied proudly.

Su giggled, but Janna, newly five and sharp as a tack, recited in a sing-song voice,

"Peter, Peter pumpkin eater

171

Had a wife and couldn't keep her.
Put her in a pumpkin shell,
And there he kept her very well."

Anne said, "It seems a bit tough on his poor wife. I hope you don't do that when you're grown up, Peter Pumpkin Eater!"

It was more a statement than a question, but Peter replied with authority. "No, I'm going to be a pirate when I grow up." If he had sought some memorable show-stopper he couldn't have done better. The eyes of the assembled Pendletons turned to him in awe.

"A pirate!" Anne repeated. "That does sound a little bit bloodthirsty, dear."

"Like Captain Hook?" Dan asked eagerly, because he had seen the video.

"No, not like him. Like Ben," said Peter calmly. "I'm going to be a pirate like Ben and fry a plane."

Twenty-one

The summer heat held the Sydney suburbs in its grip. The sultry temperatures of the day dropped only slightly with the setting sun. Even the breezes off the waters failed to make sleeping comfortable. Because there were screens across the windows to keep flying insects out, Leigh was able to leave the bedroom door ajar in an effort to create at least a pretense of draught.

Peter slept wearing a skimpy pair of cotton briefs. She chose the most lightweight of her nightshirts and abandoned as much as a sheet. Even so she slept only fitfully. Perhaps it was some night creature going about its lawful business in the gum trees which woke both her and her son almost simultaneously. Whatever it was, Peter said dopily and a little peevishly, "Mommy, I'm thirsty."

"I'll get you some water, Punkin."

The living room was cut into diagonal halves by the slanting moonlight; one half silver and soft gray, the other deeply shadowed and purple. She padded silently on bare feet, the polished wood feeling cool to her soles. A movement, followed immediately by a burst of sudden light from the kitchen area, arrested her progress.

"Oh!"

The light came from the opened door of the refrigerator. Ben was squatting on his haunches before it, delving into the back spaces of the cabinet. He turned, still on his hunkers, at her indrawn breath.

She advanced a couple of paces into the room. Ben, she saw, was wearing no more than a towel, wrapped round his lower half and tucked in upon itself. The light from the open cabinet played on his shoulders and upper arms, on the expanse of his tanned chest, on his ruffled, blond hair. He looked like a young hero from some Greek epic.

She ran her tongue over lips which were suddenly dry. The night air had been hot before. Now her skin prickled as internal heat sought the surface.

Ben straightened himself slowly, holding a can of pop in his hand. Suddenly the atmosphere was charged with the sort of breath-holding excitement engendered by a ticking bomb. He knew he must defuse things. He cast about in his mind for something, anything, which would act as a dampener. "Caught in the act," he said, like a kid found with his hand in the cookie jar. "I was hoping to catch the little green man napping."

Leigh repeated, "The little green man?"

The silence stretched like a coiled spring.

Ben cleared his throat, but his voice remained husky. "This isn't neutral territory, you know. You're beyond the demarcation line."

"I . . . Peter wants a drink."

But neither of them seemed capable of motion. Tension, like electricity, sizzled along taut wires.

"Leigh, if you stay there I might forget about being the prince. I've got a mortal side too, you know."

Still unable to move, as if her feet had put down roots, Leigh repeated, "The prince? What prince?"

"The one in doublet and hose. Velvet hat and ostrich feather."

Again she had to pass her tongue across her lips before she could speak. "You've lost me."

"It doesn't matter." Ben let his gaze linger on the shadowed shape of the young woman whose existence had rearranged the course and meaning of his life. Only four steps away, only four easy strides separated them. Under the towel which he'd casually knotted about him to cover his customary lack of night attire, his body responded to her presence in the expected manner.

She was wearing one of those T-shirt nighties again, the ones he found so very enchanting. Far more sexy than any black nylon and lace. This one was so skimpy and see-through that her every curve was silhouetted against the silver sky. He could even see in outline the V at the top of her legs. The sharp moonbeams created hollows of darkness at her throat and shoulder.

Just four steps away. And she still hadn't bolted, hadn't moved one muscle.

The words they said were unimportant. Their bodies exchanged conversation in a manner more primitive and far louder than shouting.

Ben thought, "We could do it now. I could pick her up and carry her back to my room. She would let me . . . " His virility screamed with approval at the very idea. He could anticipate how it would be, this sating of his overwhelming thirst for her. And he'd behaved bloody well, hadn't he? Didn't he deserve some reward? And by not bolting, even after his warnings, wasn't she giving tacit permission?

But then what would happen tomorrow, after his moment of heaven? Would she be demanding to be put on the first plane back to Seattle? Would she accuse him of shattering her trust? That fragile trust which he'd worked so hard to achieve. And what, in the long run, was more important?

The message of his body was plain to read, but Ben knew that he wanted more. He wanted the sort of commitment which went well beyond the immediate satisfactions of the flesh. He wanted a 'silver hairs amongst the gold' sort of commitment, a lifetime promise. And in the end that was far, far more important.

He cleared his throat, silently ordering his unruly part to remember who was boss hereabouts. "You said Peter asked for a drink? What does he want?"

Somehow she'd forgotten all about her Punkin. Somehow she'd become so caught up in the startling things which were happening inside her that his request had slipped from mind. "Water."

She couldn't remember ever before having experienced a feeling like this, not even in the happy days when she and Pete were dating; before their marriage and the hideous slide into despair. This feeling was like stepping outside her skin, a sensation of being drawn to another body by sheer magnetism. It made some inner core glow like radium in a darkened crucible. It made her come alive again.

"And you, Leigh. What about you?"

"Me?" Why was Ben talking at all, when he should

have been taking her in his arms and kissing her and . . ?

"Yes, you. Do you want a drink?"

"No. Thank you."

Ben took some bottled water from the refrigerator, poured a splash into a tumbler, handed it to her. His voice when he spoke again was the other Ben's. Not the young Greek god, nor the Nordic warrior, but Father Ben, Ben the good friend. Ben whom she trusted.

"Bloody hot, isn't it? I gather we've all had trouble sleeping."

"Yes. It's bloody hot."

He took her shoulders as he kissed her goodnight. But, although her breasts brushed against his chest through the cotton nightshirt and he could smell the sweetness of her, although in her stillness she was shouting at him, the moment had passed. The passion was under control.

"See you in the morning, then. I hope you get back to sleep without too much difficulty."

■　■　■

Leigh returned slowly to the bedroom. Peter was sleeping quietly, so she sat on the edge of her bed and sipped the water. What on earth had happened? She'd not misread his reaction. It was there plain enough to see, just by watching the movement of that towel. Then why hadn't he swept her off her feet and made mad, passionate love to her, as every atom inside her yelled for him to do? What had gone wrong?

Inside her that excited, receptive glow ebbed and waned until all that was left was a small pile of unhappy ash. She had never felt so let down, so disappointed, in her life.

And yet, when she thought about it, wasn't he just

following the rules upon which she had insisted, she had dictated?

■ ■ ■

The next day they sailed 'Boomer' out from Neutral Bay. 'Boomer,' all twenty-seven feet of her, was officially the Beresford parents' yacht, unofficially the family's. She was moored at Neutral Bay, within an easy walk of Ben's house. Her name, Ben explained, came from her red hull. A boomer was a big red kangaroo male.

They sailed west, towards the heads, and into Middle Harbor. There they moored and picnicked. Then they swam and wandered along the beach in search of shells. Once back aboard Peter settled down on a bunk for his nap, lulled to sleep by the slap, slap, of the waves against the hull. Ben opened icy cold Foster's for them both and they drank in Australian style from the bottles as the boat bobbed gently up and down at anchor. It was as though last night had never been.

Leigh was at a loss. She'd very nearly backed off from this Aussie vacation originally, because she'd assumed there would be a fair bit of coercion on Ben's part to get her between the sheets. And she knew that she was not prepared mentally for any strong arm tactics. Instead it was almost as if he'd dismissed the idea of finding her desirable, as if the only reason she were here was to act as escort to Peter.

He was actually behaving as if Peter's presence was of greater importance than hers. The child was wooed and played with, read to, entertained. Taken to the Cremorne Point pool for swimming lessons which frequently did not include Leigh. The two of them laughed together, and rolled about on the rug like seals at the edge of the strand, mock wrestling. Amazing to think that not so long ago they had eyed each other like protagonists about to engage in mortal combat over her.

Thinking it all over she could almost hear Nancy's response. "What do you expect?" Nancy would be saying, her head a little to one side in that wise-owl fashion. 'He's tried it all. Had a stab at a romp in the hay. Failure. Then he tried the good listener approach. A bit more success there. But now, now he's ready for the final assault. Romance the kid. That's what he's doing. Haven't you ever heard of luring the vixen into the trap through the cub? Your Ben, he's demonstrating that he's a pro at that."

"You're wrong, Nance," Leigh's inner self argued. "I know you're wrong. That's not like Ben at all. It's all too calculating. Too devious."

But, either way, where did it leave her? Had it not been for the evidence of her own eyes last night she'd have been forced to conclude that Ben was no longer interested in her. But only a half-wit could have mistaken the atmosphere in that room. Sparks had practically ignited their clothing.

She broached this important matter delicately and obliquely. "Last night: you mentioned the little green man. What on earth were you talking about?"

Ben squinted at her sideways. "Don't pretend you don't have little green men living in American refrigerators? Everyone knows they're the ones who switch the lights on when you open the door." He sighed his heavy, theatrical sigh. "The problem is, they're so darn slick. Try as I can, I've yet to catch one on the hop."

"That is a problem," Leigh agreed, quenching her smile. "Same trouble with American fridges, too." She sought some subtle way to leap the gap, realized that none was available and launched herself, anyway, aware that she might sound gauche. Aware that it didn't matter. "Last night, Ben. I think it would have been okay."

"Yeah?"

"Really. I've given it some thought. Come to a crossroads, I guess."

Ben repeated, "Yeah?"

She noticed that he was suddenly alert, taking notice. His eyes a little wary. And he wasn't helping her at all. Then he said, "And what exactly are these crossroads?"

The waters of the harbor rippled and shivered in the sunshine. The reflected light was so bright that Leigh wore dark glasses when they were aboard. She liked them. They gave her a feeling of protection, as if people couldn't read her thoughts if they were unable to see her eyes. At this moment she was grateful for their screening ability, and it had nothing to do with the dazzle.

"I think I'd have enjoyed . . . well . . . sex with you."

"But I'm not interested in sex." Ben's voice held a timbre she'd never before encountered. It was implacable.

"You're not?"

"No. I'm blessed if I'd go to all the trouble of getting you out here from Seattle, just for sex."

Leigh practically whispered, "Then what do you want?"

Again, there was that new, hard note in his voice. A touch of steel. "You know what I want, without my spelling it out. I want you. But not you for a quick romp in the hay. I'm after Long Term Leigh. The forever and ever sort. And I'll do without the former in order to gain the latter."

"Ben, don't say that."

"Why ever not? There's nothing new in it. In fact I'm starting to sound like a recording."

Despite the sunshine and the heat she felt herself shivering. "You know I can't. No long term relationship. I . . .

it's impossible. I explained all that."

Suddenly Ben grinned. "Okay, you stubborn woman! But no commitment, no sex. Those are my rules."

Across the water a white pelican flapped black tipped wings in lazy flight. Then it folded itself like an umbrella and plopped into the water. Leigh watched for it to resurface, its wriggling lunch firmly skewered, while she analyzed this new side of Ben.

"Couldn't we take it one step at a time?"

He still grinned at her, but she could recognize the determination behind his words. "Sorry, Leigh. That's not available on the program. It's an all or nothing deal." Then he changed the subject abruptly, as if they'd said all there was to say on that topic. "Honey, you remember that I'm flying this week? And that I'm taking you two up to Jane's for a couple of days?"

Twenty-two

*I*n a way it was a relief to be spending a few days with Jane and David. They needed some time apart.

The sexual spark, once ignited, was proving very hard to quench. Although Ben had not budged from his total package stand, although they might pretend nothing had happened, each casual touch, each meeting of the eyes, took on a new meaning. Even the small, mundane matters of daily life grew in importance. Leigh found every nerve end tingling in a manner which made it difficult to concentrate.

Ben drove them to Springwood early on the morning he was due to fly. He was back on the California route again. For him the drive was so familiar it resembled putting your hand into a well worn glove, comfortable but uninteresting. For Leigh it was as thrilling as everything else she was learning about this remarkable country.

There was the slow progress through the suburbs of the North Shore, with their English sounding names. This was followed by the delightful discovery of Windsor and Richmond, almost rural, still thick with colonial architecture and intricate, wrought iron embellishment. And all the while that incredible blueness of the mountains was advancing to meet them. Then the road wound up the escarpment and the vast, marvelous panorama of the plain was spread below. Finally Springwood came into view, small and friendly, remarkably like any such township in the American Midwest.

Jane's welcome was as warm as the sunshine. The small girls bounced about and beamed at Peter, then carted him off to inspect their play house. Ben departed after lunch, announcing that he planned to take them on a bush walk when he returned.

"That'll be the day, if he thinks I'm lugging my weight up and down those ferociously steep paths," Jane said after he'd disappeared.

They sat outside and drank iced tea while the children splashed about in a paddling pool. It was a totally child-oriented yard, Leigh noticed. Grass of the no-nonsense sort, a sand pile which overran its perimeters, a sturdy playhouse entered by a short ladder, and simple gym equipment. There were also oleanders spilling untidily about the borders and bottlebrush trees, and gums. Everywhere that sharp unmistakable scent of eucalyptus. Uniquely Australian.

Jane looked at her from under the brim of her hat. "Tell me what you've been doing, then. What've you seen, so far?"

"Everything, I guess. All the touristy things, anyway. It's been fantastic, like a technicolor dream. We went up the

Sydney Tower on the clearest day. I'd swear you could see New Zealand. And the zoo, of course. We went there on the ferry, for Punkin's sake. Then one day we took one of those little water taxis and had fish and chips at Doyles." She paused, thinking over the last few days, then concluded, "I guess the best thing was sailing 'Boomer' down to Manly."

Jane didn't even try to hide her shudder when Leigh mentioned their sail. "That boat," she groaned. "The worst moments of my life have taken place aboard that heaving weapon of torture. Dave got me aboard under false pretenses during our courtship days, in an effort to impress me. Being a star struck fool at the time, I was too craven to tell him that the sight of water slopping in a bathtub makes me ill. Three hours later I think he got the message. But, come to think of it, I had my revenge in the end."

Leigh smiled at the thought of that younger Jane, prepared to give her all for love. "How?"

Jane chuckled. "Made him take me to the opera. I happen to be the addict, not Dave. And guess which one became the habit?"

"Well, I don't know about the opera, but we adored the boat, both Punkin and I. Of course, it was a gorgeous day. Ben was insistent that we wear life jackets and all, but I never had a moment's panic about safety for either of us. Nor any queasiness. I'm just hoping we can fit in another sail before we leave."

"You'll gain bonus points with the family once they discover your enthusiasm. They'll . . . "

She was interrupted by a howl from Millie. The children, having abandoned the paddling pool, were making for the play house. Millie's small, plump legs had trouble spanning the steps of the ladder. She voiced her outrage at being left behind.

"Coming, Babe." Jane heaved herself out of the saggy garden chair and went to her daughter's aid. Some minutes later she sat herself down again. "Where were we?"

Leigh took advantage of the break to alter course slightly. "Tell me about Ben's parents."

Jane watched her small daughter's rump disappear into the playhouse. "Jack is the typical senior partner of every general practice in the land. Recently he's decided to become the patriarchal figure. If you can stomach that, he's a nice guy. Perhaps a little short on imagination, outside diagnosing rashes and notifiable diseases.

"And I consider Anne to be the next best thing to an angel. The most wonderful mother-in-law one could ask for. She's so accepting. I think she's one of those intelligent women who married instead of having a career, as they did, that generation. She's staggeringly tolerant. Of course, you've met Barbie."

"Twice. We had dinner with them the other day, as well."

"To put it bluntly, half an hour of Barbie's driveling inanities is enough to drive the average woman stark round the twist, but you'd never know it, listening to Anne. John chose her. She's her son's wife. That's what I mean, she accepts it so serenely. She accepts us all so totally. She's the core of that family, the axis about which they pivot."

Another howl came from the playhouse, followed by an indignant cry of "Mummy!" from Janna. She emerged looking red faced and cross. "Mummy, Millie's spoiling our game. She's only a baby, and me and Peter play better games. Can't you take her away?"

Again Jane heaved herself up. "It appears that rest time for the natives has come to an abrupt end." And she went to soothe ruffled feathers.

■ ■ ■

Jane was enchanted to have Leigh all to herself for three whole days. She'd liked her enormously back in California and was eager to pick up the threads of that embryonic friendship. This was not exclusively in an attempt to further Ben's cause, although that was not far from Jane's mind. It did occur to her that perhaps she could offer counseling to Leigh.

There was another, less important, reason for her wanting to spend some time with the younger woman. Maternity did have certain rewards, but it was foolish to suggest that it fed all one's intellectual hungers. Having a rational, intelligent person with whom to converse was heaven. And converse they did, as they walked to the local shops, as they prepared meals and cleared the debris afterwards. They talked as they strolled to the local playground, as they picnicked and made beds and dusted. This last was no more than a token gesture, because house-keeping was not amongst Jane's strengths.

It took a little while before anything important emerged. Jane was too professional to expect otherwise. She just prepared the ground, and waited.

■ ■ ■

They were again in the untidy, well-used garden when, for the first time, Leigh introduced the subject of Ben. As was her way, she didn't bounce straight in, but approached the subject obliquely. "Did you know the Beresfords before you and Dave were engaged?"

"I knew of them, because we lived on the North Shore, too. They just weren't in our orbit."

"Socially?"

"And more," Jane replied. "They went to a private school. Shore is one of those pukka places where the kids' names have to be put on the waiting list from birth, if not conception. I went to the local school. But John was in my year at Med School, David a year ahead. I met them then."

"And started dating?"

Jane paused to sweep Millie up and wipe her nose as she toddled past in pursuit of those bosom buddies, Janna and Peter.

"Yes. Although actually it wasn't as simple as that. I mean, I've not always been this shape, as you might remember from California, but I never did fall into the 'date of the year' category, even so. I decided pretty early that I'd probably not marry. Who'd want to date plain Jane Bowen? That's what I thought, and I was quite resigned to it, having decided that God awarded me brains, and I couldn't expect everything. Then Dave asked me if I'd go out. You know, Leigh, I thought it was probably for a bet."

"How long did it take you to discover differently?"

"A couple of dates. At first I said to myself, well, what the hell? What do I care if everybody laughs? Whatever his motives, at least I'll be able to say I dated the Divine David. But he appeared to enjoy himself that evening, and he asked me out again. I reasoned that this must be some mighty important bet, or a dare perhaps, but I was already simply potty about him. So I braced myself for the hurt, when the phone didn't ring. And, wonder of wonders, it never happened."

"And at that time Ben was still in school?"

"Just about to finish his H.S.C. That's our leaving exam, like the French baccalaureate. Vital for entry to University. Ben pretends to be dim, but he's no fool, you know. He did well."

"But not well enough for Med school? I mean, everybody else in the family is a doctor, so you might have expected that he'd become one, too."

"Oh yes, if he'd wanted to," Jane replied. "But Ben decided way back, when he was only small, that what he intended to do was to fly. It took a bit of character, sticking to his guns in the face of the family's amazement. But he had his private license well before he left school, and TransOz offered him a cadetship while he was going through Uni."

Leigh sat back in her chair with her eyes closed, letting Jane watch the children, enjoying the peace and the sunshine. From high in the gum trees two parrots squabbled half heartedly. There were other varieties of parrots up in the hills, she'd discovered; not the coastal lorikeets, but scarlet and green king parrots and crimson rosellas.

She thought about Ben, explaining to his incredulous parents that he really did intend to be a pilot and not a doctor.

Jane continued, "He's come a long way, the baby brother. And you've helped a lot, Leigh."

She opened her eyes with a start. "Me? I've done nothing."

"Yes you have, perhaps unwittingly. Let me explain. In a way it's the same with all three brothers. As if they had too many gifts, being so blessed and not really valuing them. Like good health. You don't value that until you're faced with illness. And everything for Ben has been easy. Easy career, easy sexual conquests. He never had to fight for anything, until he met up with you again. You've shown that when he encounters something important, and he thinks you and Peter are really important, he's prepared to fight. That's growth."

Leigh said slowly, "But he wants to marry me. And I'll never marry again. I've told him that. He just doesn't believe me. He seems to imagine that I'll finally give in, if he persists. He doesn't understand why I won't."

Jane's receptors moved into the alert mode. She knew that they were very near to something of overriding importance, perhaps the key to Leigh's hedge of thorns. Unfortunately another squabble was about to break out as Janna bossily excluded her small sister once more from the game.

"Do you want to tell me about it?" At Leigh's nod Jane became brisk. "Let's put these little darlings down for their naps, and we can talk undisturbed. And anyway, I can't think without my doodle sheet. We'll have to go indoors, if only for that."

Twenty-three

*I*n the study they were surrounded by David's meticulous neatness. It stood in stark contrast to the happy shambles which was the rest of the house.

Jane produced a jug of iced tea as insurance against dehydration. She sat behind the desk with her doodle pad and pen poised for action. Leigh occupied the chair from which Ben had sought Jane's aid not so long since.

Aware that getting started was often difficult, Jane broke the silence. "What about your childhood? Your parents?"

Leigh was still wondering what it was about Australians which made them such easy confidantes. Was this a trait shared by the nation as a whole, or had she happened to stumble upon an exceptional family? She looked at Jane, sitting like a buddha and positively overwhelming that desk chair. She looked at her level gray eyes and her lovely, honey-gold hair. You could sense her compassion, rather like an aura.

Leigh shrugged. "The modern nuclear family. Split, like the atom."

Jane doodled while Leigh outlined the history of the divorce, weighted, of course, towards Alice. "I have visions of Daddy, still, arriving home in his uniform. He used to put his peaked cap on my head, so pleased that I'd come to meet him. And suddenly he wasn't there. I think I'd have understood better if I thought he didn't love me, but he always seemed so thrilled to see me. The sense of abandonment was devastating. It's still hard to come to terms with, even now. I mean, if he loved me, why didn't he at least write to me, or keep in touch?"

"What about your relationship with your mother?" Jane's pen was having a fine old time, creating a row of grinning faces, like the line of clown heads at a funfair into whose mouths you post ping-pong balls.

Another slight shrug, which Jane noticed with interest. Leigh's body language said she would like to shed the whole concept of family.

"Mom believes she did her duty by me until I married Pete. Then I became a Pendleton and therefore his responsibility. Add to that the money she inherited a few years back, and I think all-in-all she finds me an embarrassment."

"An embarrassment?" Jane echoed.

"Oh, not because I chew with my mouth open; but I'm a constant reminder of those other years. The years she'd prefer to forget."

"Ah. And now you find families threatening?"

Leigh tried to assemble her thoughts. "Not threatening.

That's too strong. But something at which I'm useless. The other day when we met with them, I felt overwhelmed, and totally inadequate. I don't know how to do family."

"My dear," Jane looked up from her pad, "You are not alone. Lesser mortals than Leigh Pendleton have quailed before the combined clout of the Clan Beresford. Poor old Jane Bowen, for one."

"You, too?" Leigh said in amazement. It was quite hard to imagine anybody so secure shaking in her shoes.

Jane poured them both more iced tea. "But that's not the whole story, is it? You'd not be so determined to stay single if your fear of family was the only problem. Taken one step at a time that could be solved."

Leigh sipped the tea. "No."

Jane looked down at a veritable Medusa under her pen. The hair writhed and twisted like serpents from the head. She had a sudden vision, one of those pinpoints of insight which scramble by so fast you must be lightning quick to pounce on them.

In this vision she could picture the four of them, she and David, Leigh and Pete, at the golf club. It was one evening a long time after the engagement party. They met at the bar and stopped to have drinks. Pete, so darkly handsome and aggressively sophisticated, had asked Leigh something, and she'd replied in a youthful, careless manner. And Pete had, yes, Pete had grabbed her by the hair, dragging her head sharply back, thrusting his face into hers. He looked quite ugly in his anger. Jane waited for her to make some sort of protest, but Leigh remained silent. And there had been fear in her eyes. That was it. Fear, raw, naked and silent. That was the message of the doodles.

"Will you tell me something?" she asked.

"If I can."

"Tell me about Pete, Leigh."

Pete. She knew Jane would get there, given time. And the wounds had to be opened at some stage, examined and cleansed. She'd shut them out of sight for too long, as it was.

"Did he beat you?"

"Occasionally. When he said I needed to be taught a lesson, or reminded that he was the boss. I was going to leave him, you know. I'd reached that decision, for Punkin's sake more than mine."

"That was brave of you." Jane concentrated on her doodle. "What else would you like to tell me?"

Leigh found she was twisting the tissue in her pants pocket into shreds, just as Peter, when anxious, twisted the fabric of her jeans. "I'll attempt to explain, but you'll have to be patient with me. It's something I've tried to forget."

"We all do that," Jane reassured her. "If it's too unbearable to face we simply bury it."

"It was as if he had a limited amount of the nicer qualities, like tenderness and kindness, and he needed to ration them out. At first, when we were newly married, I received my fair share. He was gentle and considerate. But quite soon he found a new girlfriend, and established her in an apartment in Malibu. She demanded the greater portion of his nicer parts. So then, of course, there was less for me. And girlfriend was followed by girlfriend. The whole miserable time."

"And they needed to be treated well, because they could always run away," Jane agreed. "You, for the most part, were captive."

"But that was so strange. I mean I'd never seen myself as a wimpy type, yet here I was taking punishment from him which became worse and worse. And I couldn't escape. It was as if he'd cast a spell on me. That's when I began to doubt myself. Why couldn't I leave? Why did I stay? And soon I concluded that the problem wasn't Pete. It was me, and my constant need to find approval."

Under Jane's pen grew a gibbet with a figure which might have been Pete hanging from the noose. This was swiftly followed by a guillotine which boasted a monstrous, shiny blade. Drops of blood formed a pattern on the blade.

"And sex?" she prompted gently.

"The pits. Gross. Not love-making. No love at all. Humiliating and degrading. But he told me that if I loved him I'd do what he demanded. He said other girls adored it. You became used to the pain, and found it exciting. He said it enhanced your climax, if you worked on it. I don't even know how a climax feels, because I've never had one."

She was weeping now, tears quietly running down her cheeks. "I'm sorry, Jane. Do you have a tissue? Mine's useless."

"Don't apologize." Jane fished out a handful of tissues. "Tears are a wonderful release. It seems to me your problem was you didn't cry enough."

"Oh yes, I did. But for the wrong reasons. Rage and betrayal."

"And what about your hair, Leigh? How does that figure?"

"My hair. He had a thing about it. Said he'd only married me for my hair. Sometimes he'd tie me to the bed, knotting it and saying I was his slave, to be beaten if he fancied it. Mostly he'd just take handfuls and force me to kneel before him. So painful. Then he'd thrust himself into my mouth, until I couldn't breathe. I'd be gagging, and crying, and praying that it would all be over soon, before I suffocated. It was like drowning. He really enjoyed it all; gloated if I let my misery show."

"And so . . ?"

Her voice became slightly defiant. "And so the minute he was dead I went and had it all cut off. Even before the funeral. So nobody could hold me captive like that ever again. My revenge."

"Your liberation!"

"Yes. Sort of symbolic."

"And very sensible, too," said Jane with conviction. "Such short hair suits you very well." She paused, because what Leigh told her was more terrible than she'd imagined. "Leigh, have you ever been tested for AIDS?"

Leigh mopped her eyes and sniffed. "I thought of that, too. But we both tested negative, Punkin and I. Pete was many things, but not dumb. He had his health to consider. I guess he took out shares in a condom factory."

"Look what I've done!" Jane turned around her doodle sheet for Leigh to admire. The pen had gone to town. There, intricately detailed, was a tombstone topped by a very smug looking figure with great, soaring wings, which could only be a Victorian angel. "Buried him good and proper."

"Weighted down," Leigh agreed. "Under a ton of soil, never to reappear."

"Some might say dead." Jane smiled and, stretching across the desk, took Leigh's hand warmly between hers. "Better?"

"Yes, better. It helps to have it all out. Thank you."

After a pause Jane continued, "And Ben. Let's not forget him. I hope he's done nothing to inspire such horror?"

Leigh drew the tattered scraps of tissue from her pocket and held them to the light. "Look at that. Do you think it's cathartic?" She discarded the ribbons in the bin. "Ben? Oh no. He's been marvelous. Never threatening. And I was really frightened, before we came."

"And I'm right in saying that you care for him?"

Leigh looked wretched. "You're not going to believe me if I say no. I'm a rotten liar. I think he's fantastic. The nicest person I've ever known. And I'm pretty sure, now, that the sex angle would work out, given time. But . . ."

"But . . . ?"

She looked straight into the eyes of the older woman. "Jane, consider my track record: consider my parents' track record. Do you blame me for being frightened? You've read the same things I've read. History, we know, has a habit of repeating itself. And Ben will settle for nothing less than the whole package."

"So you see it as hanging on that single issue. Your ability to create something lasting? Stickability?"

Leigh cocked an ear to noises coming from the bedrooms. The first child had awoken. "In a nut shell, I guess that's it," she said.

■ ■ ■

It took a bit of thinking about, but again the doodle pad produced an answer. The possible solution to Leigh's troubles was sitting right there, in front of her.

By the time she finished her phone calls Jane considered herself an equal to Sherlock Holmes in the business of detection. The first call was to TransOz, who handed her, eventually, to the correct department. The second call was to Los Angeles, during which she mentally heard the minutes tick over and their telephone bill leap accordingly. Finally she found someone who was bright enough to explain that, sorry, the TransOz crews and Flight Officer Beresford did occasionally stay at this hotel, but not tonight. Why didn't she try the Sheraton? The Sheraton put her through, an eon later, and she realized by the fuzziness of his voice that she'd wakened him.

"Jane. What is it? Nothing wrong? No emergency?"

"No, Ben. Sorry. Nothing like that."

As the anxiety induced flow of adrenaline ebbed the void was filled with phlegm. "You do appreciate that it's four in the morning?" His voice reflected his peevishness.

"I'm sorry, Ben. But I had to get hold of you. There's something you've got to do. Are you awake enough to hear me? And to remember? It's very important."

And he listened intently.

Twenty-four

*B*en rented a car and drove south to Newport Beach. After Jane's dawn call he'd found it difficult to return to sleep, so he was feeling a bit short changed. Nonetheless, without betraying Leigh's confidence by so much as a hint, she'd also given him plenty of material for contemplation.

Newport Beach oozed money, tasteful money; from the tree-lined boulevards to the chic little boutiques where a month of his salary could easily be swallowed up in the price of one little black dress. Even Ben, who was generally blind to all such matters, was impressed.

He was immensely thankful that Leigh had not been born Leigh Smith. De St. Croix was sufficiently unusual to be a single entry in the phone book. 'De St. Croix, A.M.'

read the entry. He considered calling first, but decided to obey Jane's advice. Face to face, she'd ordered at four-ten A.M. You must look at the body language. Study everything. You can learn so much, that way. And don't stint on the old Aussie charm, baby brother.

The apartment block was impressive. No doubt about it. Those stone lions at the entrance, the palm trees, the polished marble, reflected only the finest taste.

The maid spoke with an accent unfamiliar to him. "Mrs. De St. Croix is not here. She's at the country club with Mr. Curtis."

Ben thought that they certainly guarded their riches in this neck of the woods. He explained to the guard at the fortified entrance to the club that it was urgent he speak to a member. Even then, nobody seemed able to supply him with the necessary information. It took several queries before he struck gold.

"Alice? At the court probably, watching her young man. Go down towards the lake and turn left."

Fifteen frustrating minutes later he laid eyes on the object of his search.

She was seated by the tennis court, an afghan across her knees, dressed as though the temperature were in the lower thirties, instead of a comfortable seventy-plus. And somehow, as soon as he saw her, he recognized her. It wasn't that she looked like Leigh. She didn't. It wasn't the presence of a small, silky-white dog on the chair by her. Doubtless any number of Country Club members owned similar pooches. Nor was it the merely fitful interest she was taking in the tennis match being played out before her. It was something else, an air of cozy self satisfaction which surrounded her.

Ben said, "Mrs. De St. Croix? My name is Ben

Beresford. I'm a close friend of your daughter's." He held out his hand. Alice didn't shake it. She laid her slim, limp hand against his palm, as if conferring an honor.

"A close friend of Leigh's you say. You can't be very close, or she would have mentioned you." She had that sort of pleasantly modulated voice which his mother would classify as gentlewoman, but she spoke as though her mouth were filled with cherry pits.

"Close enough for her to be staying with my family at this moment." He didn't wait to be invited to sit. He lifted the dog from the other chair and seated himself upon it. The little animal drew back his upper lip and snarled gently, with all the menace that four pounds of canine flesh can generate. "Close enough to want to marry her."

"Indeed?"

Suddenly he had all of Alice's attention. He also had the attention of one of the tennis players. Six foot two of beautifully put together masculinity said from the other side of the netting, "Do you want my help, Alice?" His voice was totally English Uppercrust.

Alice waved a graceful, beautifully manicured hand in his direction. "No, no, Curtie, dear. This young man has just told me he is going to marry my daughter. You continue with your game, but concentrate on that backhand return. It still needs some work, dear."

As the tiny dog's growls grew in volume and it looked set to mount an attack on Ben's ankle, she picked it up in a gentle, scooping motion and settled it on her lap, lowering her face to receive a cursory lick. "Pookie, Pookie. What a brave little man you are, protecting your mistress from this great big stranger. But now you must be quiet, darling. I need to talk without interruption."

Ben watched her in amazement which he hoped was

well concealed. How could this affected, caricature of a woman have given birth to someone as special, as three dimensional, as Leigh? Now he could understand that edge of scorn which crept into her voice when speaking about her mother. It was utterly remarkable.

Once Pookie had settled quietly in her lap Alice turned her attention again to Ben. "Are you a fortune hunter, Mr. Berryford?"

Ben needed all his concentration to stop his jaw from dropping in amazement. "No, of course not! And, anyway, you're the same age as my mother. Still quite a young woman. I imagine you'll live for ages." Were his mother here she would chastise him for gross rudeness, but the thought had surfaced before he could curb his tongue.

Alice looked at him severely. "I did not imagine you were hoping to gain anything from me," she said. "But my daughter is, after all, a Pendleton."

"Is that significant?"

Alice continued to regard him levelly, but there was a note of condescension in her reply. "I realize by your accent that you are a foreigner, so it's possible you are not aware of how things stand. My daughter was married to one of the Pendletons. Actually, the heir. This puts her in a very delicate situation. She will have to think very carefully before marrying again. I, personally, would not recommend it."

Ben was still trying hard not to goggle at all this. "Do you mean because she's so rich?"

"Of course I do," Alice replied calmly, gently stroking Pookie's silky hair with the tips of two fingers.

Ben had come armed with a list of things Jane thought they should discuss. His being a fortune hunter was not paramount on that list. He cleared his throat, by way of ending this particular topic. "Mrs. De St. Croix, how well do you know your daughter?"

"Very well indeed, Mr. Berrington," Alice replied graciously. "I know myself to be greatly blessed to have such a daughter. We have what I would call an excellent relationship. My friends often comment upon it, with a degree of envy. We value each other's independence and integrity. We each know we are there to be called upon in moments of trouble."

"Like losing a husband in an accident?"

The stroking of Pookie halted for perhaps three seconds. "Yes, indeed. That was such a terrible tragedy. Poor, dear Leigh. But she coped. How proud I was. Of course, that is just such a case as I was referring to. I was there, prepared to help, at any time. Dear Leigh needed only to phone for me to fly to her side." She paused to nuzzle the dog before continuing, "There would have been tiny problems. Pookie really doesn't appreciate my high-spirited grandson. Curtis would have a difficult time managing in my absence, because the dear lad is sadly undomesticated. But I'd have worked it out, somehow, if Leigh had been in need of me."

Ben thought of that tacky apartment, with its grayish walls, Leigh's depressing job, and Nancy, the witch of the west. He repressed a strong desire to throttle her mother. Instead he said, "Forgive me for asking, Mrs. De St. Croix, but are you still in touch with your ex-husband? I'd really like to ask his permission."

Alice's voice was suddenly shrill. It was sufficiently carrying to make Curtis look over his shoulder and miss his return shot. "My ex-husband? Dick? Good heavens, no. That man has been missing but not missed from my life for twenty-one years. And let me tell you this, the only good thing ever to come from that association was my daughter.

No, Mr. Bindlesford, I am not in touch with him."

"And you'd have no idea where I might reach him?"

"No idea in the world." She paused, casting him a calculating glance; then fondling Pookie's ears as she thought. "Leigh has probably mentioned that he was in the Navy. We lived in San Diego back then. But the Navy can send you absolutely anywhere. I cannot imagine why you should wish to waste your time on a wild goose chase. Asking permission indeed! But if you do," and she shrugged slightly, "You might start with Naval Personnel. They might well be able to refer you to someone else. Of course, he was probably kicked out of the service years ago, because he never could keep his hands to himself."

■ ■ ■

After he had said good-bye with as good a grace as he could muster, and was again on the road in the rental car, Ben tried to think of the questions he would have asked, had he been sitting in Alice's seat. One day he would have a daughter, his and Leigh's. One day some young man might approach him, and say, 'I want to marry your daughter.' What would he, the father, say?

Can you care for her? Will you cherish her as she deserves to be cherished? Will you fight battles for her, and hack down thorn bushes if necessary? Will you always be there to comfort her in times of trouble? Not, are you a fortune seeker?

But Jane was right in one aspect. Quite often the questions left unvoiced were as relevant as those which were asked.

■ ■ ■

Finding Alice had taken a little effort. Chasing down Dick in San Diego took half a day of his precious time. This was chiefly because the Naval people proved to be so cautious. He could understand their reserve, but each rebuff meant added frustration. Finally he went into a bar to find some sort of alcoholic comfort, and got into idle conversation with the guy behind the bar who said, "Have you tried the phone book?"

Just like that. Why the hell hadn't he thought of something so simple? Could he excuse his stupidity as being caused by lack of sleep?

There was one De St. Croix listed in the book. Captain Richard L. The phone seemed to ring for far too long. Then, when finally it was answered, a young voice called in response to his request, "Dad, it's for you?"

"Captain De St. Croix? My name is Ben Beresford, and I'm a friend of your daughter's."

"A friend of Elizabeth's? That's fine. She's here, shall I get her?"

"No, a friend of Leigh's."

"Leigh's." And the silence rose like drifting smoke

Then the voice at the other end of the line repeated, "You say you're a friend of my daughter, Leigh's?"

"Yes sir. I was wondering if we might meet. I'd like to talk to you." He held his breath.

"But that's wonderful! Of course we must meet. Come on over. Do you have anything to write on? I'll give you instructions, because this is not an easy house to find."

■ ■ ■

Even with the instructions Dick's was not an easy house to find, but the search was worth it. It was a pleasant, suburban house on the hill, with tidy lawns and gardens and a wonderful view across the bay. Clearly they had posted a sentry to look out for him, because Ben heard an adolescent voice call, "He's here," as he climbed from the car, and Dick De St. Croix hurried down the steep path to greet him, arms outstretched to seize his hand warmly and to shake it with the enthusiasm of an exuberant labrador.

"Come in. Come in." He led the way. "This is such a pleasure. How is Leigh? How is my girl?"

Several times Leigh had called her father 'a gentle man.' While his arm was being pumped, and they were ascending the flight of steps to the open doorway, Ben could appreciate her choice of adjective. He was of only average height, but trim. He had Leigh's eyes, or the masculine version of them, with smile marks at the corners. He exuded charm and warmth and welcome.

But before Ben could reply there were introductions to be made: Sally, who was Mrs. De St. Croix, Ricky and Paul and finally Elizabeth, who might have been Leigh shorn of a dozen years.

"This is Buster. Buster, shake hands." Paul was like a coiled spring, all adolescent excitement. Buster was large and shaggy and definitely a dog, but nobody would like to presume further upon his parentage. "We chose him, at the animal shelter. He was going to be put down, and we saved him."

It took a while before the general level of enthusiasm abated sufficiently for rational conversation to ensue. In the end, having extracted a promise that Ben would stay to share an early dinner with them, Dick excused them both from the family, gathered up some beer and led the way to his study. Shutting the door he gestured to Ben to take a bottle and a seat. "Now. Tell me all about my girl!"

"I'm not sure where to begin."

"We knew she was married," Dick offered, opening a bottle and pouring the contents skillfully into a glass. "Sally spotted the photo in the society pages of some paper. Frightful photo, though. All grainy. You could scarcely tell it was Leigh." He paused. "But that's not you. You're not dark like that guy, and the name's wrong. So where do you come into things?"

Ben took a long draught of beer. "Her husband was killed. A year ago. You do have a grandson, though. His name is Peter, like his father's. He'll shortly be four."

Dick's smile held a fair bit of wistfulness "Me. A grandfather? I've been a grandfather for four years?" It was clear he was thinking of that lost time. Then he laughed. "I'd better break it gently to Sal, though. She may not fancy sleeping with an old grandpa."

"I want to marry her."

Dick looked at him keenly. "Yes. So?"

"I'm not here to seek your permission, although your approval would be a bonus. But I do need your help. I met your ex-wife this morning."

"Ah, Alice. Remarkable woman."

"As you say," Ben repeated. "Remarkable."

"How was she?"

"Busy being rich."

"You don't say." He scratched his head in a gesture of mild bafflement, then continued, "But how can I help? I'd do anything, you know, to help my girl."

Ben had been thinking about how to word all that needed saying, sounding out phrases, as he drove down the freeway to San Diego. "Leigh has this total certainty about things, particularly regarding families and relationships. For her it's laid down in tablets of stone."

"That absolute?"

"That absolute. I'm not betraying a confidence when I tell you that her marriage was miserable. She has this bee in her bonnet that it was all her fault, and the fault of her genes. Your ex-wife has portrayed you in a pretty damning light, if you'll forgive my bluntness. According to her you were the Casanova of the entire naval establishment. Leigh refuses to marry me because she thinks she's like her mother. She's quite certain that our relationship will turn sour, too. And she needs to protect herself. She's reluctant to risk the hurt."

"Alice says that? She told Leigh all about my . . ?"

"Affairs. Repeated affairs. Many of them."

"Geeze." He let out a long drawn breath, studying with unseeing eyes the amber liquid in his glass. "That woman has a monopoly on vitriol." Dick looked at the younger man with the bright eyes which indicated unshed tears. "I'll tell you this, Ben, in confidence. Our marriage must have been the worst five years of my life. Of anybody's life. In a way you can't blame it all on Alice. I met her on the rebound from an unfortunate affair. Before that her father abandoned the family. Alice came to the altar bristling with prejudices, fed by her mother. She must have done a great job of spoon-feeding them to poor little Leigh. I didn't have affairs. I didn't even flirt. But Alice read infidelity into a fair hair on my blazer sleeve, the casual glance at a nicely rounded fanny. She was certain I'd follow in her father's footsteps. Alice drove me out of that marriage the way she'd driven me out of her bed. Sally and I didn't meet for another three years."

"But you abandoned Leigh, when you abandoned the marriage. That's left scars, too. Jane, my sister-in-law, says she's still seeking approval, by way of compensation."

"Not without a fight," Dick said doggedly. "Into

courts, into lawyers' offices. And the letters I wrote to her were always returned unopened, written over 'Address Unknown.' The same with all the gifts I sent. Finally, in court, the judge asked Leigh if she wanted to see me, to see her daddy, and she whispered, 'No.' I'll tell you, Ben, it nearly broke my heart."

He paused, and Ben could read in his gesture the pain which had haunted him. "But I obeyed the restrictions, did what Alice wanted. And I saw the damage it might do, if we fought over Leigh like warring tigers. I do understand that." Again he paused, while he relived those earlier years. "You know, Ben, I adored that little girl."

Ben thought about this. "She adored you, too. As far as I can tell she has no recollection of being asked about anything in court. Her perception is that you disappeared like the villain in a pantomime, never again to be heard of."

Dick roughly wiped away a tear which had spilled over. "Poor Leigh. Poor little girl. What do we do now?"

"Will you come and meet her? She's living in Washington State, right now. Bring your wife, if she'd like to come. I'll arrange it all."

"Really? She'd like to see me? Us? "

Ben's smile broadened. "I think to discover she has a family, a father and stepmother, two brothers and a sister, will be the very best Valentine's gift ever dreamed up for Leigh."

Twenty-five

Bursts of noise interrupted the chat in the Springwood kitchen. Leigh was helping Jane to clear away the children's tea things. Dave would not be home for another hour. The noise did not spell happy harmony.

Janna burst into the kitchen with all the drama of a budding prima donna. Her blond curls awry, her face was flushed with the righteous indignation which comes from personal knowledge of the truth. Behind her tagged Millie, wide eyed with uncomprehending interest. A glance through the door showed Peter in an attitude of anxious defiance. He was twisting the hemline of his T-shirt into a grubby knot, lower lip extended into a pout, brows drawn together.

"You tell him, Mummy!" Janna demanded. "You tell him. Ben's not his uncle, is he? He's mine and Millie's, not Peter's. Peter says that he's his uncle, too. Peter tells fibs."

Jane wiped her hands on the voluminous apron which draped her front and looked down at the crossly pink face of her daughter. So much passion in so small a body, over so tiny an issue. Was this the moment to try to explain honesty versus tact and kindness?

"Peter, come here, pet," she called.

Peter's steps were infinitesimal and at the speed of a reluctant tortoise. Anxiety was written into every particle of his body. Jane dropped herself down on the porch step, so that she was nearer to his level. She was aware of Leigh behind her, sensibly biting her tongue. As Janna danced on impatient feet, Peter came within range and Jane drew him alongside her. "Is it so important?" she asked, speaking only to him. His mouth still clamped firmly, his eyes overbright, Peter could only nod.

"Tell him, Mummy. Tell him." Janna urged.

"Pet, Janna's right. Ben's not your uncle," Jane said gently. "Lucky Ben, lucky old him. Uncles are people you're born with, and they have no choice whatsoever who their relatives are. Sometimes they're unlucky, and end up with nieces who are obnoxious young ladies, like Janna Beresford, for one." And she looked at that young lady, who turned, if anything, pinker and ceased to dance. "Ben's far more important than an uncle to you, Peter, because he got to choose. Do you know what he is?"

Peter twisted his shirt into an even tighter scrunch and mutely shook his head.

"He's your host, that's what he is. And that's the most important person he could be, your host, because he was able to choose you to stay with him. Okay?"

Another silent nod, but by his beam you'd think he'd just been conferred the keys of the kingdom.

■ ■ ■

The host in question appeared hot-foot on the heels of his elder brother, while the children, harmony restored, were doing their best to swamp the bathroom.

"Don't say it. I know you're not expecting me until tomorrow, but we landed an hour early, and I couldn't see any reason to go home first. I'm here to throw myself on your mercy, but if you're at starvation's door I promise I'll eat only the scraps."

"Fool," Jane said, endowing the word with new meaning by the warmth of her tone. She noticed his eyes scanning the room. "Leigh's in the bathroom, trying to stem the riot. How was your mission? Successful?"

"More than I can say. I've so much to tell you, but can it wait?"

Millie, hearing his voice, called "Unca Ben! Unca Ben!" and the other two took up the chant.

"Okay, you monsters. Have you no manners?" Ben appeared in the doorway of the bathroom.

All three children were in the tub, and so were at least twenty other items essential to their enjoyment. Leigh was kneeling on the mat, wielding a sponge the size of a man's head. She smiled up at him. He bent down to her level, wiping from her hair traces of foam which had escaped from the tub, and kissed her softly. "Missed me?"

"Missed you." It was becoming a small ritual.

"Uncle Ben, Uncle Ben, wash me." Janna was all giggles and five year old flirtation.

"Wass me too," Millie echoed.

Ben looked them over critically. "I certainly think you need some help. I've never seen three such dirty children in my life!"

Janna giggled again, her fists in her mouth. Peter, less familiar with this game, said sturdily, "I'm not dirty."

"Oh, no? Then what's that nasty brown line all round your middle?"

Peter looked down at his tummy, neatly bisected by the tan which he'd slowly acquired during his time in Australia.

"That's not dirty," he protested. "That's me."

"Oh yeah?" Ben challenged again, as the small girls watched in delight. "Just you wait until I get my scrubbing brush and scrub that line away."

"You can't." Peter looked calmly up at him. "You're not my uncle, so you can't. You're my host."

"I am?"

"Yes. Jane told me you were."

"I see."

Ben refrained, with admirable restraint, from commenting that he sounded like something out of a Eucharistic service.

So, instead of scrubbing away imaginary dirt, he rolled up his sleeves and knelt by Leigh on the mat. He blew them great and wonderful bubbles, creating a film across the 0 of his joined fingers and blowing so softly that the bubbles oozed away from his hands and lifted gently over the heads of the three children. Each bubble gleamed in iridescent suspense, each one seemed more splendid than its predecessor. Their progress was monitored with awe by five pairs of eyes.

The spell was broken by Jane's voice. "Have you all drowned, in there? Do I have to mount a rescue mission?"

"Right," Ben said. Because she was the closest child, he

plucked Janna from the water and wrapped her in the folds of the nearest towel. Janna's face emerged from the top, damp and happy, like the head of a jack-in-a-box.

"Ben?" Clearly Jane felt he'd spent enough time in there. She was agog to hear news from his trip.

He ruffled Leigh's hair. "Can you cope alone? I dare not disobey the summons. Who knows? I may be subjected to bread and water rations, and I do need to talk to Jane."

Leigh smiled in reply, while she continued to dry between Millie's plump little toes.

Twenty-six

*B*en borrowed a child carrier backpack from David, but Peter opted to use his own pair of sturdy legs. He walked manfully along the trail with them, needing scant assistance. The track Ben had chosen was not too arduous, but meandered down the tree-clad hillside over leaf-strewn boulders and bright red clay.

The air was filled with the calls of birds alien to Leigh. A strange 'whooooo WHIP' Ben identified as a pair of whip birds, Australian magpies cried mournfully to each other. Once their ears were assaulted by what sounded like maniacal laughter.

"Kookaburras," Ben said. "Otherwise known as laughing jackasses."

"They woke me the other morning, and for a few

seconds I thought I must have gone insane. You realize they're misnamed. They sound like the first Mrs. Rochester, stark, raving mad."

Half an hour down the track they turned off onto a broad shelf of almost bare rock, partially shaded by the graceful fringe of wattle and warratah shrubs. It was very hot.

"This is the top of a dried-up waterfall. It fills up in the winter only," Ben explained. He turned to Peter. "Come on, Kiddo. Help me find some dry wood for the barbie."

It was a perfect place for a picnic, even thoughtfully equipped by the park authorities with a blackened, well-used grill. No fear of fire here, in the center of bald rock. Ben had told her all about the anxiety of summer fires; not so different from California, she reminded him.

"What're you cooking?" Peter asked as Ben skillfully flipped sausages. The smell emanating from above the glowing embers made his mouth water.

"Aussie bangers. Sausages to you," Ben replied, "And chicken. Okay?"

Peter tested his new word. "Num."

The flesh tasted slightly of the eucalyptus wood which had fueled the fire. The adults drank chilled wine, they finished their repast with slices of the sweetest pineapple. The sun beat down on them from the unrelenting blue of the Australian sky. The haze shimmered. It was gloriously soporific.

After they had cleared away their things, Ben thought about the hike back. "Dave mentioned that the old trail round the waterfall, the one we used to climb as boys, was to be closed because of erosion. If you don't mind waiting here, I'd better investigate. There's no point in taking you the long way back, only to find we're on a hiding to nothing."

Leigh watched him go, admitting to herself how attractive she found the set of his back, the length of tanned, muscular leg. She thought about those incredibly brief shorts, so sexy, so beloved of Australian males. What did he call them? She wondered why nobody had marketed them back home.

She found a place in the dappled shade of a wattle tree, made a pillow out of her backpack and stretched out. From there she could watch Peter's activities in comfort. He had casually waved good-bye to Ben and returned to his favorite game of roads and cars. In the absence of any other medium he found a square yard patch of powder-dry debris and started creating an interchange of tracks with several usefully shaped twigs. He looked enchantingly serious under the floppy brim of his light cotton hat. Leigh knew that the game would keep him happily occupied for some time.

"Punkin, keep well clear of the edge, won't you?"

"Okay," Peter agreed abstractly.

She squinted up through the pattern of wattle leaves at the brilliant sky overhead. In many ways it all reminded her strongly of California, the pungent scent of gum trees, the shrill sirens of cicadas drowning out all other sound. Several small lizards brazenly sunned themselves about a foot away from her head.

She could have sworn she hadn't slept, had not so much as closed her eyes, when Peter's scream jolted her to her feet. She'd read of people saying their blood ran cold, and disregarded it as hyperbole. Now she understood with icy certainty the veracity of that phrase. "Punkin?"

He was there only seconds ago, now he was nowhere in sight. Trembling with terror she approached the edge of the dry waterfall and peered over. The small body lay about ten feet below her, on the lower shelf of the cascade bed. It lay very still and there was a trickle of blood oozing through the hair on the crown of the head. The cotton sun hat had fallen further along the shelf.

"Oh, my God. Oh, Punkin."

Her legs were trembling so violently it was hard to scramble down the side of the fall. She had to clutch at shrubs and branches to prevent her descent becoming an uncontrolled tumble.

He looked so tiny, so still. Pray, God he wasn't dead.

"P . . . Punkin?"

She knew that in accidents you shouldn't move the victim. She'd done all the first aid training years ago. But that had never involved her son. That had concerned some nameless, other person for whom you were going to perform selflessly fine, Good Samaritan deeds. She knelt beside him. He was breathing. She could make out the tiny movement of his chest and almost at the same time his eyelids fluttered slightly.

"Thank you, God." She was not religious, but she really meant it at that moment.

"Leigh? Peter?"

Never in her life had she been more thankful to hear her name called. "Ben! Help me . . . Please . . ."

Ben crashed noisily through the undergrowth and was by her side. The relief of his presence was overwhelming.

"Careful there, Kiddo. No, don't try to get up. Just lie still, for a few moments. Leigh, honey, keep him shaded while I do a spot of checking."

Peter started to whimper as his senses returned. Leigh gently stroked his brow and talked quietly and soothingly to him as Ben checked for broken limbs.

"All okay there, thank goodness. We're in luck. All these dried leaves and stuff must have cushioned his fall.

And the cut on his head isn't too serious, more of a glancing blow, I think. Although he may have concussed himself."

"What about internal injuries?"

"Hard to tell, but we'll let Jane examine him. Wearing her doctor's hat."

They set off along the homeward trail half an hour later, by which time Peter appeared to have recovered almost completely. Ben, however, wasn't deceived. "Shock. He's bound to have some reaction. I'll carry him on my back. How did he come to fall?"

Leigh, feeling that she had just proven herself the worst, most inadequate mother ever, could vouch no more than a guess. But Peter supplied enough information for them to conjecture in brief, staccato phrases about the rest. He'd been intrigued by a lizard, followed its progress, forgotten his mother's warning to keep well away from the edge.

Half way up the track he vomited violently all over Ben's shoulder.

They found a stream and rinsed the two shirts, put them on again still wet and proceeded to climb the escarpment. The second time they simply abandoned the soiled articles of clothing in the garbage bin.

Ben knew, without her spelling it out, how much Leigh was blaming herself: would probably blame herself for the rest of her life. There were no trite phrases which seemed adequate, and he wasn't about to broach the subject, anyway. What could he say? Look, you can't guard a child every minute of every day. If he's like most boys he'll do other, much worse things in his life, and you have to let him. He'll try jumping off roofs, falling out of trees, and he'll play tough, bruising sports. That's the way life is. Nobody ever grew from being wrapped in cotton wool.

■ ■ ■

Jane needed only to examine Peter's eyes to confirm their diagnosis of concussion, and added the possibility of a hairline fracture of the skull. "He'll have to be in hospital overnight, so they can Xray as well as monitor him. I'll phone ahead so they'll be expecting you."

The emergency room at the Children's Hospital was cool, the staff reassuringly calm and efficient. Leigh accompanied Peter as he was trundled off towards the Xray department. Ben paced, scanned an old copy of Sports Week, longed for something alcoholic and paced some more.

It seemed an eon before Leigh returned. She looked dust covered and drawn. "It's okay. They've found no sign of a fracture and no internal problems, either. Just concussion. You were probably right, all that dried up debris cushioned his fall."

And, for the first time since the accident, she burst into tears, giving vent to the terror and anxiety and guilt which she'd bottled inside her. Ben held her close, soothing her, comforting her by his presence, wishing that in moments like these he was not robbed of the ability to articulate all he wanted to say.

"You do realize this is my brother's shirt you're soaking," he commented some time later, as she wept against his shoulder. "Where is Peter now?"

"In his room, sleeping. They're keeping him overnight, just to be certain. Because of the concussion."

"Can I see him?"

"Yes."

They had put him into a side ward. He appeared to be hooked up to a forest of monitoring machines. The patch on the back of his head, where he had cracked it against the rock, was shaven and painted with some vividly red solution. Ben took the small hand as it lay slightly curled above the sheet, looking brown and healthy against the whiteness of the cloth. He stroked it gently with his thumb. "Do you want to spend the night here, if they'll let you?"

It wasn't Leigh who replied, but the brightly efficient young nurse. "Take your wife home. There's more than one form of shock, and I can see she's worn to death. We can look after Peter, and he'll sleep now till morning. That's nature's healing. What you both need is a good meal and some rest."

Leigh opened her mouth to protest, but Ben added his weight to the nurse's advice, and she agreed without too much of a struggle. Peter didn't need her at this moment: the thought of getting out of her grubby, sweat-soaked clothes and into a refreshing shower was very tempting.

The house on Cremorne Point was wonderfully cool as Ben unlocked the door and let them in. Only three days away, but it seemed a lifetime since they had left for the drive up to Springwood.

■ ■ ■

Leigh sat on the side of her bed and felt herself trembling. Suddenly her fingers had become thumbs, every movement became a supreme effort. She realized that tears were flowing, uncontrolled, down her cheeks. Ben found her thus when he appeared a few minutes later with long, ice-laden drinks for them both.

"Leigh, my darling, don't. Don't cry."

"I can't help it. I can't stop. It was all my fault. He'd never have fallen if I'd been watching him."

"He could have fallen if we'd both had our eyes glued

to him. Kids do. Honest." He put down the glasses and sat beside her, drawing her against his shoulder, where she continued to weep. "Darling, don't reproach yourself. It doesn't help. It happened. It's done with. We're lucky, the damage was slight. Peter will be fine, only a tiny scar he'll be able to show the other kids and boast about."

He went on telling her of the tumbles, the accidents, the scrapes in which he and his brothers had been involved, described trips to the hospital, to his father's surgery for repeated patching up. "Honestly, these days our parents would be suspected of child bashing, we were so often in the wars."

It brought not so much as a glimmer of a smile. Still, very quietly, the tears rolled. They sat in silence for a long time, while Ben stroked her hair, softly massaged the nape of her neck with his thumb, and gazed abstractly across the top of her head. He was overwhelmed with the sheer volume of the love she kindled in him. Then, very gently, he began to undress her, peeling off the grubby shirt, undoing her bra, sliding the straps down her arms.

Finally, as if just realizing what was happening, Leigh said, "What are you doing?"

"Comforting you, my love. In the best way I know how."

She allowed him to continue the process, unresisting, like a very tired child.

It was not the way he had imagined making love to her, in the many, many times when he let his imagination rip. But then, he'd never conjured up this particular set of circumstances. In his fantasies they would come together in an orgy of passion. The hedge of thorns finally hacked to the ground, Leigh willingly offering herself, and Ben in the role of lover kindling a flame which Pete had never suspected she possessed. In his dreams she was positively panting for his caresses, not lying unresisting, impassive. But what he said was no less than the truth. He could imagine no better way in all the world to offer her comfort.

He undid the buttoned fly of her shorts, laid her gently on the bed and drew the denim garment along her legs. Her panties followed. Her thighs were streaked with a film of ochre clay from the day's exertions, there were distinct demarcation lines where her body had been protected by her clothes from the dust of the bush walk. A dark circle of fine reddish soil under her breasts indicated where the edge of her bra had been. He traced it with his fingers, letting them stray over the pinkness of her small, delicate nipples.

In his dreams they would have come together squeaky clean and fresh as morning daisies, and yet to Ben at this moment there was nothing more lovely than her begrimed, streaked body as she lay on the faded linen bedspread. His anticipation resembled the countless Christmases of childhood, seeing all the gifts under the tree, knowing that they would soon be his.

He knelt by the narrow bed, kissed her gently on the lips, not even allowing his tongue to stray. Nothing threatening; nothing remotely invasive. He stroked the short fringe of hair back from her forehead.

"Darling . . . Are you okay? Is this okay?"

She lay silent and unmoving as he removed his clothes, only her eyes monitoring his progress. He thought, hoped, she registered a flicker of interest when the extent of his tumescence became evident. All the months of devotion and longing he'd experienced came together in his love making. He was slow and deliberate in his actions, tender and considerate, and infinitely loving. For the first time he discovered in himself the ability to put his partner's needs ahead of his own, to pace himself so that Leigh could join him in his pleasure.

He could understand so well, now, Jane's allegory of the Sleeping Beauty, although dust streaked and grubby as he was, it was hard to equate himself with any story book hero. And yet, he did manage to awaken her with a kiss, a very long, searching kiss, filled brimful with all the emotions he was experiencing. Leigh was able to part her lips and gain pleasure from his seeking tongue in a way which she'd have thought beyond her only days ago.

And he found a form of sanctuary between her thighs, as he entered her with equal slowness, holding his weight on his arms so that together they formed the two fingers of a wishbone. He watched the conjunction of their bodies and the arousal which grew like a summer storm in Leigh, stirring deep inside before culminating in a fusion of earth and sky. The climax arrived with a startling, shuddering speed which was completely new to Leigh and staggering to Ben. Then she burst into tears again.

Ben rolled back on the bed, which was difficult because it was extremely narrow, and looked as perplexed as he felt. "My darling, what's wrong?"

"It was wonderful. I've never enjoyed anything so much. I just don't deserve it. I don't deserve to be so happy."

He held her close to him on the narrow bed, his chin against her hair and his heart full, until her weeping resolved into sleep.

Twenty-seven

They showered, changed into fresh clothes, ate a hastily assembled sandwich and returned to the hospital. Peter had not stirred. Ben drove up to Springwood to collect Leigh's and Peter's abandoned belongings. He wondered, as he retraced the familiar route, whether by leaving those few garments and toys in Australia he could hold them hostage? The only article of any value was Peter's small scrap of much loved 'blankie'. But at least the drive gave him something to do. He felt useless when unemployed.

Leigh dozed awkwardly in the armchair by Peter's bed. She was there for her Punkin when he woke in the morning. Apart from the shaven crown of his head there was nothing to show for his mishap.

They were booked to return to the States on tomorrow's flight; this would be their last day and night in Sydney. Once Peter was discharged from the hospital, with the advice that he be kept quiet, they returned to Cremorne and filled the day with low-key, low excitement activities. In the afternoon they drove round the bay to Mossman to say their good-byes to Anne and Jack.

After Jane's comments about Anne, Leigh looked at Ben's mother with fresh insight. She had liked what she'd seen of her previously, now a fair dosage of admiration was added to the liking. This was the mother of whom she dreamed. An accepting mother who didn't demand one hundred percent perfection of her sons; who thought children should behave like children, and not like miniature automatons. And, one who could accept Barbara uncritically, because John had chosen her.

Anne, in gardening garb, fair hair escaping from beneath her straw hat in untidy tendrils, admired Peter's tonsured crown and small sticking plaster memento. She embraced them warmly, although with a certain regret. She had hoped that they were about to spring the announcement of an engagement on her.

"Come back and see us again, my dear." She kissed Leigh's cheek, smelling of soil and leaves and clippings. "And make sure you bring your pirate son. We shall miss you both. Next time round we'll all get out in 'Boomer' together."

Leigh felt unable to say that there would probably be no next time round. Discovering that she wasn't entirely frigid was one small step. Being able to accept that she found Ben vitally attractive was another. Neither step persuaded her that she could surmount the inbuilt shortcomings of her genes. That was a different ball game.

For obvious reasons Ben's plans of a final, sumptuous supper à deux atop the Sydney Tower had to be aborted. Instead, Peter safely tucked in, he fixed them a stir-fry of shrimp and Chinese vegetables, and then insisted they ate with chopsticks. They watched a comedy on the television, talked about everything under the sun except the previous evening. When he had brewed coffee they took their cups out onto the deck and leaned against the rail. It was a gentle, subdued evening. Yesterday's heat appeared to have burnt itself out. The leaves of the magnolia and frangipani trees might have been cut from black paper and gummed against the backdrop of the dusky sky. The air was sweet with the scent of jasmine.

"I mentioned that, didn't I?" Ben said. "You and jasmine, intertwined in my mind ever since Paula's party. And somehow memory and the sense of smell share the strongest link. See, I bought a vine and planted it in a tub. That way I could always come out here, smell those flowers, and think of you."

Leigh smiled. "You're such a surprise, Ben Beresford. Every time I think I really know you I discover a new facet. You're an appalling romantic at heart."

"You've discovered my soft center." He leant across and nuzzled her gently with his nose. "Now say that you like it, that caramel interior."

But Leigh's attention was diverted by a number of dim, gray ghosts flying by on shadowy wings. "Ben, What are those? They can't be owls, can they?"

"No. They're flying foxes. Fruit bats. They come in flocks from the northern suburbs each twilight, on their way to the Botanical Gardens. At dawn they fly home again. We just happen to be on their commuter route."

"But they're lovely! I'd always imagined bats would be

spooky." There was something almost magical about those silent creatures and the slow, measured beat of their flight. "And they come every night?"

"In the summer. Mind you, the people who live near their suburban hang-out mightn't share your delight. They do all their gossiping in the daylight hours. And I'm told they're a bit odoriferous. Stinky, actually."

But he didn't want to talk about the characteristics of flying foxes. He wanted to talk about the two of them. About last night. He drew Leigh to him so that her back was nestled against the length of his body, and crossed his arms over her chest.

"Watch out. You'll have coffee all over me."

"Finish it. Or abandon it." He snuffled against the smoothness of her neck, gave her ear a tiny nip, then whispered against it. "Leigh, and summertime and Sydney. My version of the perfect triangle."

Leigh did not reply.

Ben continued, "Are you going to spend tonight in my room? Are you brave enough to cross the demarcation line?"

He could feel the slight stiffening of the girl within his arms. "Ben . . ."

He pretended not to notice, gave another small nip of her lobe, let the exploratory tip of his tongue investigate the outer shell.

Leigh said, as if it explained the meaning of life, "I talked to Jane."

"Wonderful woman, isn't she, my sister-in-law?"

"She's a marvel. And she's helped me so much."

"But?"

"But I have to think. There's a lot to be sifted through, and so much garbage to discard. Do you understand?"

He kissed the hollow of her neck. "I'd understand a

great deal better in my bedroom. My powers of comprehension are bound to be at their best there."

"Ben, no."

"Really?"

"Please. Everything went on hold with Punkin's accident. And how can I sort it out when you're kissing my ear? So I need to put some distance between us. I have to be away from you to get everything straight."

"That's the most hopeful thing you've said to date."

"But do you understand? My need to think everything through?"

Another kiss on the nape of her neck. "This place is going to be so empty in twenty-four hours. I don't think I'll let you go, tomorrow. I'll kidnap the pair of you and hold you captive here, forever."

Leigh said in a flat voice, "I've already had a taste of that, being held captive. It's not a bundle of fun."

Ben accepted defeat graciously, as he had known he would from the start. "Okay, Leigh. Let's be sensible. Next week, we fly into Frisco on Wednesday. It's the last flight before the schedule changes. Who knows where I'll be after that? Anyway, I'll get myself onto a shuttle to SeaTac. So arrange a baby-sitter. Okay?"

"Sure. There's Jill, or Nancy if she's still around. Did I tell you that she has a new man? His name is Keith, and he's a trucker for one of the lumber companies, down in Portland." She paused. "And Ben . . ."

"I'm still here."

"Thank you for everything. We've had a marvelous vacation, Punkin and I, if you disregard his accident. And that was my fault. You couldn't have done anything better, at any time. I just wanted to say that."

Ben was reluctant to release her. He planted one last

kiss on the hollow of her throat. "Dearest one. It was easy. Ask me again, any time."

Twenty-eight

*S*eattle in late January. Everything dripped; the branches of the trees, the overhang from roofs. Her nose.

It seemed all the more dreary because the Christmas decorations were down. Leigh found the grayness to possess a certain soothing quality, but it stood in stark contrast to the brilliance of Sydney in midsummer. She settled back into doing all the routine things which were the pattern of her and Peter's lives.

Peter, newly four, started at his play school, and returned home after two hours' separation brimful of enthusiasm, and bursting with a dozen items of news to share. Leigh was grateful that he should take the transition so easily, but wished with a part of her mind that he missed her, just a little bit.

She also did a great deal of thinking. Ben would be in town next Wednesday. That was something to look forward to. After that there were twenty-two days until February the twentieth. And after that?

He phoned her from San Francisco, as was his habit, to tell her that the flight was on time, to put on her glad-rags. "We're going to be eating out tonight. Friends of mine who'll be in town. I'd like you to meet them."

"Oh." She wondered who the friends could be. Paddy O'Hare sprang to mind, but wouldn't Ben remember that she knew Paddy? Wouldn't he mention him by name? Anyway, the good news was that she had a new dress to wear, one she'd seen in a boutique in Kirkland and bought for just such an occasion.

It was a gorgeous dress. Green, with a hint of gold in the pattern of peacock feathers. It was a bit lower cut than she was in the habit of wearing. The neckline flirted with the edge of her shoulders. From there the dress clung to her figure, in at the waist, smoothly over the hips before the skirt flared a little. She could wear her gold chains and matching earrings.

Jill, when she arrived to baby-sit Peter, gave it the thumbs up. "That is a gorgeous dress, on one gorgeous figure," she said admiringly. "Why on earth do you hide a shape like that in pants and sweaters?"

"Protection." Ben's arrival saved Leigh from explaining what she meant.

"Perhaps we could cancel the evening," Ben said. "Just stay at home, the two of us?" She took that as approval. Then, to spare her blushes in front of Jill, he continued, "I've got a birthday present for Peter. Let me say goodnight to him and we'll be on our way."

Once they were on the freeway he said, "Of course, I come weighed down with a thousand messages. Barbie and Mum, and Jane. Janna has drawn a picture for Peter. I fell out of favor by saying it was a tremendous koala. Janna looked hurt and explained that it was supposed to be a kangaroo. Anyway, you made a hit at home. You know that, don't you? John wanted me to explain why I let you escape without an engagement ring on your finger."

"Oh. That's nice of them all." Such warmth was a bit overwhelming. But she, too had news to share. "Ben! I met Nancy's new guy. We went out, the three of us, to a Karaoke evening. He's the most enormous man you ever met, built like the Incredible Hulk, with muscles bulging everywhere. And tattoos. You've never in your life seen such tattoos."

"Is that admiration I detect in your voice? Shall I sprint to the tattoo shop tomorrow and have 'Ben loves Leigh' inscribed across my behind? With a dragon or two?"

"Don't be silly. But that's not all. I mean, he's the toughest thing you ever saw, but when we got to the bar he's up there with the mike in his hand before you can blink an eye, singing 'White Christmas.' Isn't that totally bizarre?"

"You want me to add serenading you to the list of desirables?"

"Of course not. But Ben, 'White Christmas?' And there's Nancy, who's spent her time warning me about the pitfalls of marriage and the evils of men, positively drooling over him. I tell you, it was an amazing evening. And now she and Ryan are off to Portland to live with the guy."

Ben said, "Suddenly I quite like old Nancy."

He parked the car in the underground garage of the Olympia Hotel. As they waited for the elevator she sensed that his mood had changed. There was a tautness about him; a sense of anticipation, a bit like that time aboard 'Boomer'.

Could these fellow diners be someone important to his career? Someone like Tibor Szep?

The feeling heightened when, as they waited for the elevator to arrive, he kissed her softly and said, "Leigh, honey, I just want you to know that you are the most wonderful thing ever to happen in my life. You and Peter, both. Remember that, always."

Leigh wondered what he meant as the elevator whisked them towards the lobby. Not his words, but his tone. She'd rarely heard him sound so serious.

They stepped out into the lobby, all thick pile and polished marble. Leigh scanned the scattered groups of people, seeking someone she might recognize, someone perhaps with the bull-shoulders of the great and mighty chairman of TransOz. Nobody remotely like that caught her gaze.

There was one couple, standing by a pillar, who looked a little familiar, but . . . Her eyes snapped back to the man. He wasn't particularly tall, nor particularly striking. He was balding a bit, and wearing an ordinary gray suit. But he did have very nice eyes.

Her voice was no more than a whisper, and it broke at exactly the moment that the man turned and noticed her. "Daddy?"

About twelve yards of luxuriously carpeted foyer separated them. As Sally commented later, it was like watching one of those ads, in which the couple start apart, and close the intervening gap in ultra-slow motion. One wonders if they will ever get there. But meet they did. And Leigh was in Dick's arms, and there was a confusion of 'Daddys' and 'Leighs' as if they had forgotten each other's names, or needed further practice in saying them. And quite a few tears.

Sally, looking elegant and neat, turned to Ben. "What do you say to buying me a drink?" she said a little briskly, because there was quite a lump in her throat, too. "I have a feeling that the script at this moment says, 'Ben and Sally exit right'."

■ ■ ■

Sally sat in the lounge with one trim ankle crossed over the other and sipped her martini. "In the absence of the principal players I think you might count this evening a success."

Ben grinned at her. "With your help. It can't have been easy for you having someone out of Dick's early life re-manifest herself. You had to be prepared to accept Leigh, too."

"That wasn't hard. Of course, I knew all about that disastrous first marriage, and Dick had always told the children, so there was no surprise sister sprung on them. In fact, the hardest part was persuading Elizabeth that this was neither the time nor the place for her to be. We placated her only by promising that we'd persuade Leigh to visit San Diego in the near future, bringing Peter. And Paul rushed off to school with wings on his heels to announce that he's actually an uncle."

Ben glanced at his watch. "How much longer should we give them? Leigh must be running out of tissues."

"Long enough for me to ask you this: I assume that if or when Leigh marries you, you'll be taking them both to live in Australia?"

"If. She still has to agree. But, yes. Commuting across the Pacific is no easy matter."

Sally sighed. "It does seem a pity, for Dick and Leigh to

meet after all this time, only to be separated by half the world."

"But there are certain advantages which go hand in glove with working for an airline," Ben pointed out. "Cheap fares, for one. And there's also the consideration of Peter and his other grandparents. He'll always need access to them. I think you might say that the world is smaller than you imagine."

He looked up as Dick and Leigh, hand in hand, approached them. Both were beaming, but Leigh looked decidedly smudgy.

"Isn't she lovely, Sal? My daughter? Isn't she just the loveliest girl?"

Sally stood to hug Leigh. "Of course she's lovely, Dick. What else would you expect?"

"And I've been telling her how lucky it was that Ben found us. Home only three months in San Diego, after all those years being posted round the world. And now the bonus of a grandson, as well! Christmas come late."

Sally said, "He's been impossible to live with, these last few days. And the children. Leigh, I must extract a promise from you that you'll visit us very soon. Very soon indeed, or Elizabeth will self-combust with frustration. She's spent her life longing for a sister."

She looked at Leigh's streaky face. All those tears of happiness had not done a great deal for her make-up. "Now, my dear, what do you say to our visiting the powder room? These men can be smug together, while I get to know a bit about my new daughter. Then we must have dinner, or I, for one, will faint from starvation."

Twenty-nine

hey left the hotel fairly late because there had been
so much to talk about, so much time to make up.
There were photographs to be inspected and admired,
snapshots of the three half-siblings in San Diego, those of
Peter which Ben just happened to have in his wallet.

Leigh was still dazed. She needed to have it all repeated
several times, while she sifted through the chronology. "And
you visited my mom, first, while I was still at Springwood?
You drove down to Newport Beach?"

"That's right. Had a delightful and informative chat.
Met Pookie, too, and saw the estimable Curtis, without
actually having the pleasure of a formal introduction."

"And all this was Jane's idea?"

"To quote your first president, 'I cannot tell a lie.' She

woke me with the first birdsong to give me my marching orders. But after that I was on my own." He found himself grinning like a hyena. Leigh's excitement was catching.

"I can't believe it, yet. It's so fantastic. Yesterday there was just me and Punkin, or the two of us and Mom, if you must. Today I have my father again; and a whole family. It's mind boggling."

"Was he as you remember him?"

"Yes. A bit less hair, but essentially he hasn't changed. He's such a . . . such a . . ."

"Gentle man."

"That's it. And you like him, too? And Sally?"

Ben squeezed her hand. "Yes. I think he's one great bloke. And Sally, too. She's smashing."

"Can I say thank you? Thank you for going to all that trouble, just for me."

■ ■ ■

Jill fully understood the lateness of the hour, under the circumstances. Peter hadn't stirred. The TV was showing all repeats, as usual. There was nothing of interest to report.

After her departure Ben removed his tie with relief, unbuttoned his collar and poured them both brandies from the bottle which he had conveniently brought.

"Come and sit here."

He put his arm round her shoulders. His fingers tugged gently on her ear lobe, then moved lightly, exploratively down her throat, outlined the neck of her dress. One slid under the fabric and traced the edge of a lacy strap. "You look wonderful tonight. I like this dress. I like what's inside, too." And then, after a decent interval, "Have you followed Jane's wise words? Sorted things out?"

The alcohol was warm inside her, like embers. Not that she needed further warmth, she realized, because she was still on a sensations overload. And she'd done a great deal of sorting out, disposing of mental garbage.

"Yes. Yes, I have. Ben, will you be patient?"

Ben drained the last of his glass. The disappointment was like being doused by a bucket of cold water. He very nearly groaned. If the events of this evening had not been sufficient to level the hedge of thorns he knew he'd run out of ammunition.

But Leigh stood and took his hand. "Come with me." She led the way along the passage to her bedroom, scarcely noticing that his slap-in-the-face look had been replaced by one of bemusement. It was a very tidy room, Ben noticed. Neat, like its owner. Cream and blue. No scattered pantyhose and abandoned articles of clothing.

"Sit down."

Still slightly dazed, Ben did as he was told, on the low, padded chair she indicated. With suddenly awkward fingers he fumbled towards the buttons of his shirt.

"No. You still don't understand!" Leigh was fierce in her determination. "I told you, I need you to be patient. *I* want to undress you. It's so important to me, Ben."

He grinned with delight, wanting to say something encouraging but not daring to, for fear of spoiling the moment. "Be my guest."

In her mind she'd rehearsed this, taking each step very slowly to make sure she did it right. She knelt before him and disengaged each button, then put both hands behind his neck, spread her fingers and peeled the garment away, over the shoulders, down the arms.

Then she knelt back on her heels and looked long and hard at his body. Not the quick glances in the past, when she'd thought herself unobserved, but a thorough study of the line of neck and shoulder, the curve of the muscles across the chest, the fuzz of blond hair. Kneeling up, stretching, she ran her fingers through his hair and explored the shape of his ears. She drew with one finger the line of his lips. Then she took his head between her hands and, pulling him towards her, kissed him, tracing with her tongue the edge of his teeth, skimming across the smooth enamel. The brandy fumes mingled in their mouths.

When the kiss ended she knelt back again and continued her exploration, down the chest, pausing to investigate each nipple, to let her fingertips travel over the stomach, invade the dent of his navel.

"You can help me with your pants." Ben did.

He wore the briefest underwear she'd ever seen. If their task was to keep him decent they were doing a very limited job. Leigh slid her palms down his hips and into the fabric. "Help me."

"In a strip tease you have to use velcro," Ben remarked in the voice of another person, but Leigh wasn't listening.

His manhood stood to attention, hard and tight against the flatness of his stomach, embedded in its thatch of light brown curls. Leigh ran her hands along the muscles of his thighs while she kept her eyes strictly on his groin. "You know, I've never done this before," she said quietly. "Not ever."

Ben didn't want to think of Pete. There was space in this room for only the two of them. But he also recognized its importance to Leigh. He was feeling like two people, anyway. There was an intellectual Ben rejoicing in this demolition of the hedge of thorns, and another guy who was entirely physical, the excitement of whose body demanded his undivided attention. It was no contest, could never be.

The physical guy won, as Leigh leaned forward and continued her exploration, using her tongue. Then, a few minutes later, with tiny nips of her teeth. This time he did groan with delight.

"You like that?"

"Don't ask!" Ben replied, almost unrecognizably. "Don't stop."

She gave small, delicate sucks, while her tongue continued its work.

Presently Ben said hoarsely, "Is it my turn? I can't hold on forever. Can I undress you?"

"No. But you can watch."

She stood and peeled off her clothes as if she'd been born a dancer in an exotic land. The green dress slid to the ground, then hose, bra and panties. The only thing missing in this erotic display was the music, and the throb in Ben's head provided rhythm enough. Then, bare and beautiful, at the moment when he thought he could accept this passive role for not one second longer without self-destructing, she parted her thighs, straddled his and very gently pinioned herself on his staff.

He steadied her back as once again she took his head between her hands and kissed him, again allowing her tongue to invade his mouth. When, finally, he could speak, he said with all the emotion that one word could contain, "Leigh."

And then they were silent.

Ben, in his elation, registered her climax, aware of the moment by the glazing of her eyes, the arching of her back under his supporting hand, her stillness. And when he followed it was with a spasm of rapture which dwarfed anything his imagination had ever conceived.

"You see?" Leigh was exultant when, some minutes

later, the rapture had been replaced by a glow. "Not you invading me. I had possession of you. I was in charge, in control."

Ben's grin was one of unrelieved pleasure. "My darling, I don't care what you call it. Just be prepared to do it again." He picked her up and laid her on the bed. "Now it's my turn to explore."

■ ■ ■

Some while later, in the small hours of the morning, when their hunger for each other had finally been sated and they were lying contentedly entwined, Ben said, "I wonder what happened to that other girl, the one at Cremorne who was so impassive when I made love to her?"

"I think we've buried her tonight, along with the frigid one, and a great box of bad memories."

Ben looked at her tenderly. "No, that's wrong. Not a burial. This was a funeral pyre, fueled by the chopped-up thorn branches. Finally hewn to the ground."

"Ben Beresford, there you go again. You're forever coming up with remarks I don't understand. Like calling yourself a prince. Remember? Now thorn branches. What are you talking about?"

So Ben told her.

"Me? Sleeping Beauty? Scarcely." But she smiled at the thought. "I think I was more like Rapunzel, trapped in a tower."

"How could you be Rapunzel?" Ben protested. "Look at yourself. Her hair came to the ground, remember?" And he kissed her again. "And while we're in confessional mode, I have another confession to get off my chest. Do you remember that accident Pete had, at your engagement party?

That was me. I was that accident. He ran into my fist."

"You?"

"I barged into a bedroom, thinking it was the bathroom. And Pete was busy laying this blond bird. I kid you not. All fru-fru hair and big tits."

"Marcie? Marcie Wagoner?" interrupted Leigh. "Pete was in the bedroom with her? But she was my friend, she worked with me. He'd never seen her before that evening."

"So? Anyway, I was still busy being dazzled by your smile, and I was so mad at him that I socked him one. There. I have bared my soul and told you all."

Safe and serene within his arms, Leigh could giggle. "Ben, that's marvelous. Don't you realize, you got your revenge way, way before me."

Thirty

*N*ancy was in the midst of relocating and Leigh was helping her. They were surrounded by all the paraphernalia which goes hand in glove with do-it-yourself moving. Peter was at his pre-school. Ryan was underfoot and whiny, because he found the whole business thoroughly unsettling.

Nancy had been extremely interested in the discovery of Dick, in the newly found brothers and sister, although Leigh had forgotten to mention Ben's role in the drama.

"I'm taking Peter down there, to San Diego, for the long weekend. I'm going to have to learn 'family.' Take a crash course, I guess."

"It isn't so hard. You start with an advantage. They'll like you, and you don't have to fight over the bathroom, or emptying the dishwasher, like ordinary families. You'll get along fine, believe me."

They carefully lifted another crate of packed utensils into the truck. Tomorrow Keith would come up to drive the truck to Oregon. Nancy would follow in her old jalopy, although her fiancé had promised her a new car as a wedding gift.

Nancy was taking a great deal of care with furniture which, in Leigh's opinion, was fit only for instant removal to the dump. She could understand it from Nancy's viewpoint, though. These sorry pieces of furniture were hers, and hers alone. They had seen her through good and bad times. They would be there as an insurance policy if things didn't work out with Keith. Nevertheless, she was embarking on this new phase in her life with quite a lot of optimism.

"Whatever happened to Nance the Misanthrope?" Leigh asked, as she paused from her task of wrapping plates and assorted dishes in newspaper.

Nancy straightened and rubbed the small of her back. "Well, you know, she's still lurking in there, waiting for a chance to get out. But we have to go forward, don't we? You can tell me I'm being dumb, and I'll agree with you, but there it is. Who was it that kept Hope to herself, out of that box? Pandora? I'm like her; holding onto Hope, while keeping my back to the wall."

Leigh said admiringly, "Fancy you quoting Greek myths."

"And what about your cutie?" Nancy asked. "You haven't had much to say about him, since the vacation in Australia. Is he still around?"

"Yes, I think so."

"But you're not so sure?"

Now that Nancy had abandoned her self-appointed

role of President of Emotional Addicts Anonymous, Leigh felt she could tell her a little more about Ben.

"He's been flying to Japan, this month, but . . ."

"Okay, kid. Tell your Aunt Nancy."

"I thought everything was fine, until about three weeks ago. That was the last time he was here. Usually he phones from wherever he is. This month I've heard nothing. Nothing at all. Not even a postcard. And . . ."

"And?" prompted Nancy.

"Nance, do you remember those roses you asked about? Months ago?"

"Sure. Two white ones and a bunch of pink."

"They were to remind me of a date. February the twentieth. The pink roses were the days, the white ones the months. That was the date he said he'd be asking me to marry him, and he wanted me to have time to get used to the idea."

"You don't say. I'll give the guy marks for originality. Anyway, what's the significance?"

"Nance. Today's February the twentieth. And I don't have the slightest idea where he is."

"You're thinking he's cooled to the whole idea? Or that you should be sitting hunched over the phone, waiting for it to ring?"

"Hardly. No, I'm prepared to help you pack. It keeps me occupied. But . . ."

Nancy was happy to give her aching back a rest. She sat down on the nearest packing case. "What will be, will be," she said with a marked lack of originality. "Ryan! Will you quit that whining?"

Leigh was grateful to take time off, too. She picked Ryan up, set him on her knee, and wiped his nose with a tissue.

"You're going to love living in Portland, near your Grandma, Rye-rye. And in half an hour you can come with me to get Peter from preschool." She comforted him, understanding very well his feelings of uncertainty and his need to hold onto things familiar. "Perhaps we'll stop at MacDonald's for a snack?"

Ryan stopped whining and said, "Keith's got a 'normous truck. I getta ride in it."

"That's great."

Five minutes later they were returning to the task in hand when Nancy glanced up and called, "Leigh! Come quick."

Leigh came out of the apartment in response to the urgency of her tone. "What?"

"Look."

She followed the general direction of Nancy's gesture. Against the uniform grayness of the winter sky a small plane was making itself manifest. Behind it flew a banner of some length. It was too far away to ascertain exactly what it said, but it was approaching rapidly.

"Well, I never." Nancy squinted up towards the plane. "Didn't I say it? You gotta give that guy marks for originality."

The banner was becoming clearer by the second. In bold red letters it read,

MARRY ME-LEIGH

then it turned a wide semicircle, so it was heading back towards the north end of Lake Washington, and the reverse side of the banner could be seen.

PLEASE!

"Mom, what's it doin'? What does it say?" Ryan asked.

"It's for Leigh. It's her man, asking her to marry him." She turned impatiently towards Leigh, who was standing as if rooted to the spot, watching the progress of the small craft. "Well. What are you waiting for? Answer him."

"What do you mean?" Leigh was still watching the plane as it began another circle over Kirkland. "He couldn't hear me."

"Fool!" Nancy was quite cross at such stupidity. With one hand she seized one of the elderly sheets which were doing double duty as dust covers and packing material, and with the other a can of spray paint which was minutes away from being discarded in the garbage can. "Answer him."

Leigh was still standing like one transfixed. "What do I say?"

Nancy nearly shook her. "How should I know? Yes or no? You tell me."

"I can't . . ."

"Oh yes you can! Hope, Leigh, Remember? It stuck with that Pandora, when everything else flew away. Now, answer him. QUICKLY."

Leigh took the can thrust into her hand and looked blankly at the ancient sheet which Nancy spread with hasty hands over the cement driveway. There was a pattern of greenish leaves on it, and small purple flowers. The can of paint, she noticed irrelevantly, was shocking pink. She could imagine no use for such a ghastly color.

"Leigh, WRITE!"

Leigh looked again at the can of paint, and then up at the plane. She had a sudden vision of Ben behind the cockpit screen, Ben with his brown legs and his white teeth and sun-bleached hair. And along with him, like a package deal, there was Sydney, and the house on Cremorne Point, and Anne and Jane, and a long line of days stretching towards the future. There was love in the package, and trust, and a great deal of hope . . .

She pressed the small button on the top of the can, and sprayed the largest shocking pink letters the sheet would allow.

YES

Then the two women held out the corners and let the cloth billow in the air, while Ryan danced a war dance and whooped with delight.

Epilogue

And so they were married, the prince and his bride. That is the correct way for all fairy tales to end.

The ceremony took place aboard a schooner called the 'Highland Lass,' which was available for charter. It sailed down the harbor one glorious, autumn afternoon, carrying the Clan Beresford and as many friends as could be accommodated. They repeated their vows to each other as the wooden decks creaked and wind filling the sails caused the canvas to luff and crack.

Peter was the best man, a task for which he was eminently suited, having achieved his fourth birthday. The ring, his responsibility, was pinned for safe measure to a hankie. Paddy O'Hare performed the other duties generally assigned to the best man, such as proposing a toast to the happy couple. He managed to play his role to perfection.

The three small Beresford nieces accompanied the bride with equal charm and success. There was no need for them to wipe the tear from her eye or strengthen her resolve to go through with the ceremony. All that was way in the past. They were joined by Elizabeth De St. Croix, excited to be there and thrilled by everything her sister did and was.

Ben would have liked Leigh to wear the special red dress. Leigh pointed out that, outside of China, scarlet was probably the most unsuitable color one could imagine for a bride. She chose, instead, to be married in a simple dress of ivory silk, and to carry a small bouquet of creamy flowers, into which were slipped some sprigs of late-flowering jasmine. Her hair had grown enough to curl softly round her face.

To her eternal chagrin Anne Beresford cried during the ceremony, something she had certainly not been tempted to do at the marriages of either of her other sons. Nor was it because Ben was her baby, or her favorite. It was more, she explained to her husband, to do with the rightness of it all. They were simply so right for each other. They made, with Peter, such a delightful trio. So complete.

Of course, the De St. Croix family all flew over for the occasion. Dick gave Leigh away, almost, he commented, before he'd had time to find her again, let alone come to know her. Nonetheless, his pride in his daughter was sufficiently evident for it to inspire in Anne a fresh trickle of tears.

Alice De St. Croix declined their invitation most graciously, being afraid to leave Pookie. She sent them as a gift a very large and extremely ugly object made out of glass. Nobody could decide exactly its purpose. In the accompanying card she called Ben 'Brian'.

Also on the invitation list was their Good Fairy Tibor, but such were his business commitments that he was unable to come. He did, however, make up for his absence by sending the sort of check which caused a sharply indrawn breath of surprise from the recipients, and made Paddy O'Hare cast another quizzical look at the totally respectable person of Anne Beresford.

At the reception they did all the things necessary to make such occasions memorable. Time honored customs were observed, such as tossing the bouquet and drinking the health of all and sundry. They ate and drank too much, remembered and repeated tales far better forgotten, laughed long and heartily. By the time it was all over, and the 'Highland Lass' was once again at her berth in Darling Harbor, the night had drawn in. Peter was to return to Springwood for a few days with Jane and David, while his mother and new step-father honeymooned at Port Douglas. They were booked to fly north the next morning.

It was strange to return to the house on Cremorne Point without their Punkin. After all the preparations, the excitement and build-up to the wedding, it felt a little bit of an anticlimax and oddly quiet. But there was chilled champagne waiting in the refrigerator. It was guarded in their absence, no doubt, by the little green man. They took their filled glasses out onto the balcony.

The last of the summer jasmine still scented the air, and in the night sky a fine crescent moon hung like a filigree ornament. The waters of the harbor were somber and unguent, the far shoreline a dark smudge. A lone fruit bat flew by on shadowy, silent wings.

Ben put his arm about his new bride as they leaned against the rail. "It all went okay, didn't it?"

"I think so. Everybody seemed pleased."

"But what about you, darling? No moments of searing panic? No regrets?"

"None. I promise."

"And you're happy? That's the most important thing. Forget about everybody else, they can look after themselves. But it's so important to me. I need to know that you're happy."

Leigh leaned against him, drawing warmth from his body in the cool night air. From the circle of his arm she said, "I promise you, Ben, I've never felt so happy in my life."

She turned her head to smile at him, her thousand-carat smile. It lit her face, it lit the Sydney night. It lit his heart.

About the Author

Sally Ash was born in New Zealand, and has also lived in Australia. These days she divides her life between homes in England and Washington State. She has raised a family of five children, countless cats, dogs and small furry animals, and taught English for many years. The inspiration for *HEDGE OF THORNS* came from her love of folk stories. Fairy tales are as old as the hills and as modern as tomorrow. Sally believes that in many ways they reflect our everyday life. When not writing, she cherishes her husband, Bruce, makes gardens and plays killing bridge.

At present she has a second novel completed and is working on a third, set in New Zealand.

Introducing

THIS TIME

by

MARY SHARON PLOWMAN

It was late, nearly eleven, and every muscle in Caitlyn James' body hurt. Did they really need to skate that last set? Probably not, but it was fun. They didn't need the pizza and pop either, but it was too late for regrets. Plenty of time to pay for their sins in the early morning light.

Cait set her overnight bag down on Jackie's bed and dug for her pajama set. Finding it, she tossed her nightshirt and shorts on to the growing pile of toiletries, cosmetic bag, and slippers. She placed her paperback on the nightstand. Most likely wouldn't get much reading done tonight, but even a paragraph or two would relax her. That, plus the hot bath, next on her agenda.

The lace curtains danced lightly in the night breeze, drawing her gaze. The window behind the love seat was open, just as it had been on that very first night. It seemed like years, rather than just weeks ago.

She flexed her neck and shoulders. Sure, she'd be stiff tomorrow, but not nearly as sore as Jake would be. During the first hour or so, he had spent more time on the floor than he did standing up. But he wasn't a quitter. Thank goodness the skating rink rented knee and elbow pads.

Grabbing her toothbrush and paste, Cait headed towards the bathroom. The lodge was beginning to feel like her second home. Jake's invitation to stay overnight and hike together tomorrow had taken her by surprise. Based on the look on his face, he must have surprised himself, too.

This emotional roller coaster was hard to deal with at times. Their relationship alternated between hot and cold, and would most likely stay that way until her decision was made. Hopefully, that would be soon.

Leaving the door slightly ajar, she set her personal items on the sink and chose a towel from the linen closet. When she bent to turn on the bathtub faucet, her leg muscles reminded her again that she wasn't getting any younger.

Straightening, she sat on the tub's edge. "Ouch." She gingerly rubbed her hip and positioned the towel under her, before sitting again. The handle marked 'Hot' was cranked up another notch.

Maybe she should have skipped the women's speed skating contest. After all, there was no way to beat Rose, but it was fun trying. Almost as much fun as watching Jake stand for the first time on his in-line skates. What a good sport he was.

A soft knock on the outer door interrupted her thoughts. No way was she going to stand, unless it was a true emergency. "Who is it?"

"Mom, can I come in?" Cait recognized her daughter Lynn's voice.

"Sure. I'm hiding behind Door Number Three."

She expected a sarcastic retort, but didn't get one. Oh well, Lynn was probably as tired as she was. Within moments her daughter peeked in and quickly scanned the bathroom. Finding the coast clear, she stepped inside.

Cait glanced around, too. This was silly, of course she was by herself. She shut off the water, noticing Lynn's hesitant movements. "What's up?"

Lynn closed the door quietly, but firmly, behind her. "Not much. What are you doing?"

Cait looked down at the bath bubbles and suppressed a snappy comeback. Something was definitely wrong. She pointed to the empty space next to her. "How about sitting with me for a minute? I'm moving kind of slow tonight." She gingerly stretched one leg. "I'm not as young as I used to be."

"Don't give me that." Lynn sat down. "You still out-skated Jackie and me."

"Now I'm going to soak away all my troubles."

"I heard the shower running earlier. I thought you were already through for the night."

"No. Maybe Jake was showering." She tested the water.

So did Lynn, swirling her hand through the bubbles instead of meeting Cait's eyes. "Oh, then he's already in bed?"

Cait glanced at her daughter's face, which was devoid of

all expression. What was the point of that last remark? As she continued to watch, Lynn's gaze roamed. First it lingered on the shower curtain, then on the bottle of conditioner. Anywhere but eye-to-eye.

Cait stood and walked over to the sink. Maybe facing away would make things easier. "I don't know if Jake's in bed or not. Didn't you see him downstairs?"

"No."

She fiddled with her toothbrush and tried again. "Then I guess he's out for the count. In fact, I'm surprised the three of you haven't dozed off by now."

"Rose and Jackie are snoozing. I couldn't sleep."

Cait made an inquisitive sound and continued brushing her teeth. Unobserved, she watched her daughter in the mirror.

Lynn chewed her thumbnail for a moment, then continued. "I've been thinking a lot about you lately." She cleared her throat and raised her voice a notch. " . . . you and Jake, I mean."

Their eyes met for a moment in the mirror, before Lynn looked away. She reached over and fiddled with the water, turning it from hot down to warm. Cait gave her daughter another wordless prompt, then lowered her head and began to rinse.

"About you and Jake and sex, actually."

Cait's head immediately shot up. Their eyes met again. Bad timing, being caught with her mouth occupied. She raised a single brow.

"Well, we've been talking and . . . we wouldn't be totally shocked, you know, if you and Jake . . . you know." Cait raised her other brow. Lynn forced out the rest. "If you did it."

Cait quickly spit in the sink. Not wanting to waste time

on a cup, she swallowed a handful of water. She grabbed the towel nearby, then turned. "Did it?" Amazing how much meaning could be packed into two little words.

"Yeah."

Leaning against the sink, Cait folded her arms across her chest. "That's quite an announcement. You caught me at an unfair disadvantage."

"Yeah." Lynn smiled shyly. "But at least I was able to say it without interruption. It's kind of a touchy subject, you know."

"I know. That's why parents are supposed to be giving their kids 'the talk,' and not the other way around."

"Well, what I meant to say is that it'd be all right if you thought you were in love." Lynn glanced up at her. "Are you in love?"

"I can speak only for myself." Cait looked at her daughter seriously. "I am. But that doesn't mean I know how this will all turn out."

Lynn nodded. "There's a second thing." She picked up the bath oil and began fidgeting with the cap. "You have to be safe. I mean, well, it's been a long time since you were in high school, Mom. I thought you might be due for a refresher course."

"High school!" Cait took the bottle and placed it back on the shelf, then sat down beside her. She coughed in an effort to cover her outburst. Just thinking of her own straight-laced school years, when skirt hems had to touch the floor while kneeling, made her want to laugh. When she finally spoke her voice was calm, gently serious. "Well, darling, it's kind of like riding a bicycle. It's hard to forget how."

"Mom, I'm talking about diseases and protection and stuff like that. Not how to's. I . . . just take these, okay?" In

260

frustration Lynn fumbled in her pocket, then produced a handful of foil packets. She dropped them into her mother's lap. "Here."

Gulping for air, Cait gazed down at the assorted styles and colors. Her eyes widened. "Where did you get these?"

"From Jackie." She shrugged. "They hand them out at our school, too, but only if you ask. In L.A. I think they come with your school books when you register."

They both sat perfectly still, staring at the pile. Lynn was the first to break the silence. "I love you, Mom." Her voice was unsteady. "I want to be able to . . ." A deep breath, "To love you for a long time."

Silence. Amid the steam and stifling heat, Cait was frozen into position.

Lynn stood. "That's all."

Cait's head cleared instantly. Jumping to her feet, sore muscles and condoms forgotten, she pulled her daughter into her arms. She squeezed her tight and rocked slowly back and forth. "I love you too, honey." She stroked her daughter's long blond hair, then kissed her. "You don't have to worry about me, okay? Believe it or not, the same information makes its way to adults, too."

Lynn's voice was beginning to relax. "Really?"

"Really."

Cait drew back until Lynn was arm's length away. Looking into her daughter's eyes, she saw her first smile of the evening. She returned it, then lightened the mood. "Hey, we're going to talk about this same topic during one of our retreat workshops. Do you want to co-teach with me?"

"Heck no." Lynn stepped out of her mother's arms and backed towards the door.

"Maybe pass a few of these around the circle?"

"Mom!"

"Maybe the group has a favorite? We could take a vote."

Lynn reached the door and opened it quickly. "You wouldn't."

"I might."

"I'd die." Lynn stepped into the hall, still shaking her head.

"No you wouldn't. You did fine with me." Cait's voice softened.

Lynn walked away, signalling a time out with her hands. "I'm out of here." She bolted down the steps.

Cait closed the bedroom door, turned, then leaned against it. A smile slowly curved her lips. "Fine, darling."

Goodfellow Press/ *Hedge of Thorns*
7710 196th Ave NE, Redmond, WA 98053-4710

1. How would you rate the following features? Please circle:

	readable				excellent
Overall opinion of book	1	2	3	4	5
Character development	1	2	3	4	5
Conclusion/Ending	1	2	3	4	5
Plot/Story Line	1	2	3	4	5
Writing Style	1	2	3	4	5
Setting/Location	1	2	3	4	5
Appeal of Front Cover	1	2	3	4	5
Appeal of Back Cover	1	2	3	4	5
Print Size/Design	1	2	3	4	5

2. Approximately how many novels do you buy each month? _____
   How many do you read per month? _____

3. What is your education?
   - ❏ High school or less
   - ❏ Some College
   - ❏ College Graduate
   - ❏ Post Graduate

4. What is your age group?
   - ❏ Under 25
   - ❏ 26-35
   - ❏ 36-45
   - ❏ 46-55
   - ❏ Over 55

5. What types of fiction do you usually buy? (check all that apply)
   - ❏ Historical
   - ❏ Science Fiction
   - ❏ Romantic Suspense
   - ❏ Mystery
   - ❏ Western
   - ❏ Action/Adventure
   - ❏ General Fiction
   - ❏ Time Travel/Paranormal

6. Why did you buy this book? (check all that apply)
   - ❏ Front cover
   - ❏ Back cover
   - ❏ Like the setting
   - ❏ Know the author
   - ❏ Like the ending
   - ❏ Purchased at an autographing event
   - ❏ Liked the characters
   - ❏ Heard of the publisher

For current Goodfellow Press updates:

Name: _____

Street: _____

City/State/Zip: _____

We would like to hear from you. Please write us with your comments.